For the bees and the bears

'Moon Bear is absolutely amazing. It seemed so real and I felt that I was with them in the book. I would recommend it to everyone in the whole world and they would definitely be missing out if they don't have it on their bookshelves.'

EVIE, AGE 10½

'This is one of the best Gill Lewis books yet. It is one of those books that you just can't put down. I would recommend this book to anyone who is looking for a journey of thrill and excitement.'

HARRY, AGE 12

'Moon Bear is one of the best books I have ever read. I could not close my eyes for a single moment of this amazing, brilliant and excellent book. The describing of the story is so good that I feel like I'm actually there.'

EVA, AGE 8

'I rate this book 10/10. Gill Lewis gets you attached to the character and makes you feel sympathy for them which is great because when bad things happen you can't put the book down because you want to make sure the character is okay.'

BEN, AGE 13

THE FIRST STORM

My grandfather and father were Bee Men. They could talk to bees. They understood them and their ways.

On moonless nights, they would climb the smooth bark of the Bee Tree to collect wild honey. The bees told them everything: where to hunt for wild game, when the forest fruits had ripened, and when the rains would come.

Grandfather always told me that we could learn much from bees.

On cool winter evenings when the rain would funnel up from the valleys and spit and fizzle in the fire, I'd pull a blanket around me and sit close to him.

'Tell me the story of Nâam-pèng,' I'd say.

Grandfather would smile. 'Nâam-pèng? Who's he?'

'Nâam-pèng, the bravest bee.'

'Pah!' Grandfather would say. 'He was only a small bee. Hardly worth a mention.'

'Please tell me,' I'd beg. 'Tell me the story of Nâam-pèng.'

Grandfather would wrap a betel nut in a leaf, and chew it slowly. 'Ah, well,' he'd say. 'Ah well.'

I'd pull my knees up under my chin and stare into the fire and watch the flames leap and dance and tell the story too.

'Long, long ago,' Grandfather would begin, 'when the world was bright and new, a Great River came flowing down from the White Mountains. This river brought forests filled with tigers and elephants, moon bears and sun bears, clouded leopards and marbled cats, mousedeer and macaques and weaverbirds and . . . ' Grandfather would take a deep breath, ' . . . so many animals, I would not live long enough to name them all. These forests reached up to the sky and caught the rain clouds in their branches, and soon there were many rivers flowing into the Great River, all of them teeming with fish.'

'But a monster came, didn't it?' I'd say. I loved this part.

Grandfather frowned and nodded. 'But one day a monster came. Tám-láai came in the dark before the dawn, striding through the forests, eating the animals and trees, spitting bones and pith onto the ground. He devoured anything and everything in his path. The animals ran and flew and swam for cover deeper into the forests, but still the monster came, tearing up the ground and drinking up the Great River so it became no more than a trickle, and the fish were left flapping and dying in the mud. By the end of the day, there was only a straggle of trees clinging to one small mountain. "Please leave us this forest," the animals squawked, and hooted and barked and squeaked. "It is all we have left." But still, the monster was hungry. He pulled himself up to his full height . . . '

When Grandfather got to this part, I would stand up and flap my blankets, throwing giant shadows out behind me. I'd take a deep breath and roar, "'I am Tám-láai. I am Tám-láai and I dare anyone to stop me.'"

Grandfather would pretend to cower. 'All the animals hid together. Not even the tiger or the bear were a match for this monster. But just as Tám-láai reached to tear the nearest tree from the ground, a small bee flew out from the forest and buzzed in front of Tám-láai's face.

'"I am Nâam-pèng," said the bee, "and I will stop you."

'The monster caught Nâam-pèng in his paw and threw back his head and laughed. "You?" he cried. "You are so small. Your sting would be no more than a pimple on me."

'Nâam-pèng buzzed inside his paw. "I am Nâam-pèng and I will stop you."

'Now when the other forest bees heard Nâam-pèng speak out so bravely, their hearts filled with hope and courage. Could they be as brave as Nâam-pèng too?

'Tám-láai bared his teeth and held Nâam-pèng by the wings. He stared deep into Nâam-pèng's eyes. The sky darkened all around them. "You are nothing, little bee, nothing. It was not your bravery that brought you here, but your stupidity. Is there anything you wish to say before I crush you with my paw?"

'Nâam-pèng quivered in fright but he looked the monster in the eye. "Tám-láai . . ." he said.

'"Speak up," roared the monster. "I can hardly hear you."

'"Turn round," said Nâam-pèng. "You must turn round."

'"Turn round? Me?" snorted Tám-láai. "As it is your final wish . . ."

'The monster turned.

'Before him swirled a huge black cloud. A storm of angry bees filled the whole sky, from end to end, blotting out the sun.

'Tám-láai crumpled to his knees.

'"I may be small," said Nâam-pèng, "but I am not alone. Did you not hear the bees?"'

CHAPTER 1

I scooped a handful of small stones and closed my fist, crushing the sharp edges deep into my skin. *Stay awake, Tam. Don't sleep. Don't sleep.*

I looked across at Noy lying on the rock ledge beside me. His head had flopped forward into his arms and he was breathing softly. I wanted to wake him. It was dangerous to sleep in the forest. Sleep loosens the souls and lets them wander. They could be coaxed away by spirits while he was dreaming. We wouldn't want our souls to wander far tonight.

I rubbed my eyes and breathed in deeply, filling my lungs with the cool night air. Above, the moon had traced an arc across the sky. We had been waiting all night. The bright star of the Dragon's Tail had risen above the tree

1

line. The forest was dark and still. This was the dark before the dawn. The dark when spirits walked.

I wriggled forward and peered down from our high rock. Moonlight reflected from the wide pools below the waterfall, the ripples spreading out in perfect circles of bright, white light. The sweet scent of moth flowers drifted across the water. The whole forest was deep in sleep. Maybe Noy was wrong. Maybe it wouldn't come tonight.

I stared into the folds of darkness on the far side of the river.

In the deep shadows between the rocks and boulders, a darker shadow was stirring. I twisted a loose piece of forest vine though my fingers and watched. Despite the coolness of the night, my palms ran slick with sweat. I could feel the blood pumping through my hands. I swallowed hard. Below, some fifty paces away, the shadow moved. It formed, gained shape and stepped out into the moonlight.

I jabbed Noy in the ribs. 'Wake up!'

Noy's head jolted up. 'What?'

'Shh!' I said. 'It's here. It's here, now.'

Noy wiped the sleep from his face and leant out. He looked down to the river and gripped my arm. 'Where?'

'There.'

Moon Bear

The shadow rose up on its hind legs and sniffed the air.

I held my breath.

A bear. A huge bear. I'd never seen one before. It was taller than Pa. Taller even than the chief. The crescent of white fur on its chest was bright against the dark fur of its body. It sniffed the air again, its small round ears twitching in our direction. It was a bear of the Old Stories. A Moon Bear. A Spirit Bear. Crop Eater. Man Killer.

Right here.

Right now.

I pressed myself into the rock. We were downwind, wrapped in shadow. The thunder from the waterfall drowned our noise. Yet, as we lay still and hidden, I wondered if this bear could sense us somehow. Did she *know* we were here?

Noy tensed up beside me. I could hear his breath, soft and shallow. I could feel him watching too. The bear dropped onto all four paws and leant forward into the river. She dipped her head low and drank, gulping the water, her ears swivelling backwards and forwards.

I breathed out slowly.

Noy leant into me. 'I told you she would come.'

I looked down to the river.

The bear was thin. She'd eaten our crops and broken into the feed store. She'd put fear into all the mothers of the village. Yet no one had managed to catch her. Grandfather said she was clever, and dangerous too if she had cubs. I thought of Ma. If she knew I was here trying to take a cub, she'd kill me.

'D'you really think she's got cubs in there?' I said.

Noy nodded. 'Your grandfather says she must be feeding cubs, otherwise she wouldn't risk coming so close to the village.'

No one had seen a bear for years. Grandfather said they'd been hunted into the deep forests. But he'd seen one once when he was young. He'd seen a bear push a man down and tear off half his face. Bears were more feared than tigers.

Noy grinned, his teeth white in the darkness. 'We'll get a hundred US dollars for a cub. Maybe more. Just think, Tam,' he said, 'not even my brother could find this den. We'll walk back to the village like men. I can't wait to see my brother's face when he sees *me* bring back a bear.'

The bear sniffed the air again and set off, jumping from rock to rock, using the river as her path down to the village fields.

Moon Bear

Noy thrust a small flashlight in my hand. 'Go!' he said. 'Go now.'

'I thought we were going in together,' I said.

Noy shook his head. 'One of us has to keep watch.'

I tried to press the flashlight back in his hand. 'I'll keep watch,' I said. 'You go.'

Noy scowled, his face half hidden in the moon-shadow. 'I found her. I found the paw prints in the mud and the claw marks in the trees, so that means you go and get the cubs. Besides,' he said, as if deciding the matter, 'you're smaller and will fit between the rocks.'

I glared at him. We were born the same night, under the same moon. We were twelve rains old. People said we shared our souls like twin brothers. Yet Noy was the chief's youngest son. He always got his way.

'Go on,' said Noy giving me a shove.

'What if she comes back?' I said. I looked along the river. It was a long straight stretch, stepped in waterfalls. The bear was swimming away from us in one of the deep pools.

'She'll be ages,' said Noy. 'There's a hundred dollars waiting for us in that cave.' He leant into me, his mouth curled in a smile. 'You're not scared are you?'

'No,' I snapped.

'So go,' he said. 'If I see her coming back, I'll warn you.'

I held the flashlight between my teeth and gripped the vines in my hands. I scowled at him. This wasn't about a bear at all. It was about Noy wanting to get one up on his brother.

I lowered myself into the river gully and stood on a rock and listened. I strained my ears into the darkness. A light breeze sifted through the canopy of leaves above. Frogs chirruped from the slack water and puddles at the river's edge. I knew I wouldn't hear a bear. Grandfather said you never hear a bear. They walk like spirits through the forest. You cannot out-run, out-climb, or out-swim it. You must become still. You must become like a spirit too.

The river was low. The rains had yet to come and fill the river gorge with tumbling fast water. I stepped across the domed rocks to the far side, to the deep shadows of the bear den.

What if there was another adult bear inside? What if the cubs were big enough to fight?

I glanced back up the steep ravine. I couldn't see Noy but I knew he was watching me. Maybe this would be one dare too far. I switched on the flashlight. Its light gave a dull yellow flickering glow, barely enough light to see. It was Noy's brother's and I guessed Noy hadn't asked to borrow it.

I edged my way into the entrance to the den. A low tunnel sloped upwards, deeper into the rocks. The ground beneath was damp and earthy. The rock walls were cool to touch. I felt my way forward. The narrow passage opened out into a small cave, just big enough to fit a bear. It smelt clean and fresh as if a channel of air flowed through from the outside.

I shone the light around the empty space. The cave floor was strewn with dry leaf litter and shredded twigs and branches. The soft earth was hollowed and coated in a layer of black fur where the bear had lain curled up, asleep. I traced my fingers through the dry leaves and could feel the warmth from her body still in the ground.

I jumped.

Something had moved.

Something squirmed beneath my hand.

I shone the light downwards. Half hidden in the leaves, a black shape stretched out a stubby paw. Small eyes blinked in the torchlight. A bear cub, no bigger than a piglet, nuzzled towards me, poking out its flat pink tongue. I stared at it. The mother must have been starving to leave it here, alone, unguarded.

It wriggled onto its back, showing the crescent moon of white fur on its chest. A whorl of white hairs above the crescent looked just like the evening star.

I couldn't take this bear cub. Could I? It was still feeding from its mother. It was much too young.

I stared at the cub. A hundred dollars. Fifty dollars for Noy's family and fifty for mine. It was more than Pa could ever earn selling honey and bush meat. Maybe we could even buy a buffalo.

Somewhere outside a gibbon called into the night. It sounded far, far away. Deep inside the cave, it was quiet and still, sealed from the outside world. The cub was safe in here. Held. Protected.

Maybe I'd tell Noy there was no cub. It didn't seem right to take it.

But a hundred dollars! We'd never get this chance again.

The gibbon called again, a high alarm screech. Something had rattled its sleep, but I felt strangely safe inside the curved walls of the den. I ran my finger along the soft belly of the cub.

Another screech, more frantic this time. A warning.

I jolted upright. My heart thumped in my chest. Noy's warning, a gibbon's call.

Moon Bear

The mother bear was coming back.

I grabbed the cub by the loose skin at the back of the neck and groped my way along the passage. She shouldn't be back. Not yet. Noy said she'd be a long time in the fields. Why had she come back so soon?

I stumbled out of the cave into the hard black body of a bear. I tripped and sprawled on the rocks, losing my grip on the cub.

The mother bear spun round. She bent her head and snuffed her cub, glaring at me with her small dark eyes. She was so close I could feel her, smell her, and hear her breath. Her lips peeled back to show the yellowed canines in her jaw.

I wanted to press myself into the ground and become rock too.

I closed my eyes. *Become spirit. Be still, be still, be still.*

I waited for bear teeth around my skull.

But nothing happened.

I opened my eyes. The bear was standing on her hind legs, her attention fixed on something in the valley. She sniffed, the tip of her nose reaching high into the air.

'*Uff!*' she grunted. A warning from deep inside her chest. '*Uff!*' She dropped down and picked up the cub. It dangled from her mouth by its scruff, its paws curled beneath it. The mother bear leapt across the river into the shadows and was gone, leaving only spreading rings of light where her feet had touched the water.

Noy crashed down from the rocks above and crouched beside me, his face pale in the moonlight. 'I thought you were dead.'

I tried to sit up but my arms and legs were shaking.

'Come on,' he said. 'Before she comes back.'

I shook my head. 'She's gone. She heard something down there. It scared her.'

Noy stood up and looked down towards the village. 'Maybe my brother's out with his gun already.'

I pulled myself up beside Noy and clung to him. We stood side by side, straining our ears into the night.

A rumble sounded from far away across the mountains.

'There's something else,' I said. 'Listen.'

Noy frowned. 'Thunder?'

The distant rumble grew. It rose up from the valleys. The groan of engines rolled out across the still night air. The echoes sounded hollow, bouncing across far hills where loggers had already started to clear the forest.

It was a mechanical grinding, tearing through the night.

Noy gripped my arm and turned to stare at me, wide-eyed in the moonlight.

There was no thunder.

This was no storm.

Noy ran his hands through his hair. 'They're coming, aren't they?' he said. 'They're coming to take us.'

I felt sick and hollow deep inside.

They shouldn't be here. Not yet.

Maybe if the rains had come early, they wouldn't have made it this far. Maybe their trucks' wheels would still be sliding and spinning in thick mud far below. But there had only been two days of hard rain. The long dirt road winding up from the great Mekong Valley was dust dry again. There would be nothing now to stop them.

The soldiers and their trucks would be here before the dawn.

CHAPTER 2

Ma grabbed me by my shirt. She held the oil lamp up to my face. 'Tam! Where have you *been*?' She glared at Noy, taking in his muddied clothes and the hunting knife strapped round his waist. She knew us too well. 'Bear hunting is not a game for boys.'

Pa pushed a bamboo cage into my hands. 'There's no time for talk. Cage the chickens before they scatter to the forest. The piglets too.' He turned to Noy. 'Get home, Noy. Your brother is looking for you.'

The rumble of trucks was louder now. They were in the valley below. I could see them, a snake of headlights through the trees. The throb of their engines pulsed through the ground beneath my feet.

Moon Bear

Sulee was wiping sleep from her eyes. Mae was crying, holding on to Ma. 'Hurry, Tam!' Pa gave me a shove. 'There is not much time.'

I grabbed the cage from him. I knew where I'd find our hens. They'd be tucked in their night roosts, in the dirt hollows around the wooden poles that held our house high off the ground. The piglets would be dozing in the warm ashes of last night's fire. In the darkness, I could hear calls and shouts from other houses. Babies cried. Pigs grunted. Footsteps and hushed voices rushed past as the village was shaken out of sleep. An escaped piglet squealed behind me, its hooves drumming the dry dirt. I pulled our hens out and bound their feet with twine so they could not fight on the long journey ahead. I pushed them flapping and clucking into the cages. I tried to grab the old cockerel, but he was already awake and flew up to the roof where he threw his head back and announced the dawn that was yet to come. Maybe he'd heard the soldiers too.

'Tam!' My father was beside me. He bent next to me and closed the cage door, binding it with twine. I could hear his breath whistle through his teeth as he bit the ends. 'Your mother and sisters are going to fetch what they can from the fields. We must pack everything. There is no coming back.'

I felt bile rise inside me, the bitter taste sharp inside my mouth.

Pa lifted the cage from me and carried it to the roadside where baskets, bags and cages, and boxes were growing in a steady pile ready to be packed into the trucks. Villagers streamed between their houses and the roadside, like a nest of forest ants on the move, holding outsized belongings above their heads. I carried out our rice bags and pots and pans. I rolled our clothes inside our mattresses and blankets. Nothing could be left behind. We would need it all.

I climbed the steps one last time to fetch Ma's embroideries. She hoped to sell them in the markets when we moved to our new home. Our house was empty now. A single room. A shell. It smelt different. Felt different. Hollow. Empty. Where our mattresses had lain was now bare floor. We would not sleep here or eat in this room again. I tried to push the thoughts from my mind. I slumped down and hugged the roll of embroidery against me, breathing in the sharp tang of dye.

'Come to say goodbye?'

I spun round. I hadn't seen Grandfather. He was sitting by the window, perfectly still, pooled in moonlight.

I pushed hot tears from my face. I didn't want him to see me cry.

Moon Bear

'I'm not going with them,' I said. 'I'm staying with you.'

Grandfather said nothing. He lit his pipe and I watched the first puffs of smoke rise like a pale blue mist around him. The sweet flower smell of his pipe-smoke filled the room. He leant back and stretched his bad leg out in front of him, the groove of the thigh-length scar dark against his skin.

I waited for him to speak, but he turned his head to the thud of feet on the steps outside our house. The door flung open and the chief held up a lamp, its circle of dim yellow light darkening the night.

I leant back into the shadows and hoped he wouldn't see me. Through the open door I could see the monster shapes of trucks, and the silhouettes of soldiers spilling out into the village.

The chief stepped towards Grandfather. 'Puan,' he said. 'The soldiers are here to take us. No one can be left behind.'

Grandfather took his pipe from his mouth. 'You know I cannot come.'

The chief paced to the window. 'You have no choice. They will burn our homes to make way for the road to the new dam.'

Grandfather eased his bad leg underneath him. 'Your father and I once fought side by side for our freedom, and yet now you give it away on the promise of a parcel of land and a new home.'

The chief turned to face him. 'That was forty years ago, Puan. Times have changed. The world has changed. We must change too.'

Grandfather leant forward through the screen of smoke. 'This is not the way.'

I dug my nails into the roll of cloth. I shouldn't be here, listening to Grandfather speaking out against the chief.

The chief leant against the window frame and stared out into the darkness. I couldn't see his face, but his shoulders were slumped. 'I do this for our children, Puan,' he said. 'We will have schools and hospitals and good homes. The big dam will give us electricity. Our country will be rich. We will be rich. Our children will lead better lives. Isn't this what you want for them too?'

Grandfather got to his feet and leant out of the window. He spat onto the ground below. The air pulsed with the throb of engines. It shook the timbers of our house. It filled the night. A million trucks it seemed.

Grandfather shook his head. 'This was once the richest land in the whole world. It was called the "Land of a

Million Elephants".' He turned round to look at the chief. 'But I do not think there are many wild elephants in Laos now. Do you?'

The chief backed to the door. 'You will die if you stay here.'

Blue smoke curled around Grandfather and swirled out through the window, as if the forest had already claimed him for itself.

'Then I will die as I was born,' Grandfather said. 'I will die free.'

The chief stared at him, then turned and left, pushing past Pa on the steps outside.

Pa saw me in the shadows. 'Tam, it is time to go. The trucks are waiting.'

Grandfather stood up. He tied his hunting knife around his waist and picked up a small bag of belongings at his feet.

I stepped beside him. 'I will stay with you.'

Grandfather held me by the shoulders. 'This forest is no place for boys.'

I gripped the slingshot in my pocket. 'I can look after myself. I can look after you too.'

Grandfather leant down. 'Tam, your mother and sisters need you more than I do.'

Pa stepped forward and took my arm. He and Grandfather stood facing each other, heads bowed, almost touching. That's how I remembered them, the last time I ever saw them together. Pa and Grandfather, the Bee Men, and a silent language passing between them. The secret language of the bees.

Outside I felt the heat. It seared through the air. A plume of thick white smoke rose up from the houses at the far end of the village. Flames reached up into the sky, the sparks drifting high above our heads into the blue dawn light. Acrid smoke hung in the air. It filled my lungs and stung my eyes. Between the flames, the soldiers moved, silent figures in the roar of fire, burning what used to be our homes. Beyond the fires, the trucks were waiting. Pa grabbed my arm and pulled me with him. The chief was standing with a soldier at the tailgate of the last truck.

The soldier ran his eyes down names on his clipboard. He looked up. 'We are missing one. There should be one more.'

Pa glanced at the chief and then the soldier. 'There are no more.'

The soldier read out a name. 'Puan Vang.'

Moon Bear

Grandfather's name.

The chief cleared his throat. 'Puan is a dead man.'

My stomach clenched. I fixed my eyes on the soldier's sheets of paper. He tapped the end of his pencil against Grandfather's name. He twirled his pencil round his fingers, as if he was letting them decide. I waited for him to tell us we were lying, but instead, he crossed a hard line through Grandfather's name, threw the clipboard in the back of the truck and barked at us to get in too.

I put one foot on the tailgate and the soldier heaved me in. I sprawled on the floor beside Ma, Sulee, and Mae and a cage of chickens. I felt feet land next to me as Pa and the chief climbed in. Two soldiers sat at the back of the truck, their guns resting between their knees. The tailgate slammed shut and the truck rumbled into life. We lurched forward and picked up speed, bumping down the track.

I glanced at our chief. He looked small next to the soldiers, not like our chief at all. Black soot smeared his clothes and skin. He stared down at his hands, his face hidden in the shadows.

When the soldiers first came, our chief said we would not move. But more soldiers came a second time with General Chan and other men in suits from the city. We were promised new homes, electricity, televisions, paddy fields, and a school. We were promised better lives. And when the soldiers came a third time, the chief agreed that we would move.

Grandfather said the chief had sold our freedom.

Pa said he had no choice.

I sat up and stared beyond the soldiers. I searched for our house but it was lost in the blaze of white heat.

Ma tried to pull me back. 'Don't look, Tam.'

But I couldn't help it.

I had to look.

I watched our village burn, engulfed in smoke and flame.

In my mind I saw the mother bear with her cub, fleeing through the forest.

Maybe one of my souls escaped with them that night, because it felt as if something deep inside had been ripped apart. I knew that nothing would ever be the same again.

CHAPTER 3

'Welcome,' said General Chan. 'Welcome to your new life.'

I sat with Noy and the other villagers on the bare patch of earth at the village edge. Our new village lay in the Mekong Valley between the distant blue hills and the great river. It had been seven days since we had left the mountains. General Chan had come to see us, clattering out of the sky in his helicopter with his men in suits and a man with a huge camera. The General stood in front of us, a short well-fed man, the buttons of his uniform straining over his round stomach. Behind his gold-rimmed glasses, he looked at us with small quick eyes.

Noy leant into me. 'He's the one building the dam, the one who made us move.'

I felt General Chan's eyes linger on us. I nudged Noy away. 'Shh!'

General Chan pushed his chest out and thrust his shoulders back. He paced up and down, watching us all. 'I hope you have now settled in the new homes that have been built for you. I'm sure you will agree they are bigger and more comfortable than your old homes.'

I looked beyond him to the houses that stretched out in two neat rows along the road. The houses were wooden, like our old homes, but set up high on concrete posts. Our house was big, but the chief and his family had the biggest house. It was nearest to the water pump, although I knew Noy's mother didn't like it there. Water spirits had already taken one of her babies. She didn't want them taking any more.

General Chan swept his arm towards the rise of ground beyond the village. 'You have vegetable gardens, and paddy fields,' he said. 'You will be able to grow enough rice to sell at the markets. You have everything you need to start a better life.' He paused and smiled. 'But come,' he said, signalling to the chief. 'People don't want to hear this from me. They want to hear it from you.'

The chief joined the General and faced us too.

The General pointed to the cameraman. 'Tell the people of Laos what life is like in your village,' he said.

Moon Bear

Noy leant into me. 'We're going to be on TV!'

The chief cleared his throat. 'It is much better here,' he said. He kept looking from General Chan to the camera. The General smiled and pointed to the camera.

The chief started again. 'Life is much better here,' he said speaking to the camera. 'We have land to plant our own rice. We have clean water. We will be able to sell our vegetables at the market. Our children will be able to go to school. We will have health care too. It is better here.'

General Chan kept smiling and nodding as the chief spoke. When the chief had finished, the camera swept across us and we waved and grinned. I had to pull Sulee down to stop her dancing. General Chan announced that he had some gifts for us all. Each household was to have two more sacks of rice. He said he had a present for the chief too. Noy's older brother went to fetch it from the helicopter. I could tell the box was heavy by the way he arched his back to carry it. Everyone watched as the chief peeled back the wrapping and opened it.

Children in front of me knelt up to see.

Noy turned to me and grinned. 'Just look at that!'

I watched as Noy's brother lifted out a huge television. I'd only seen one through the window of the bar at the logging station where Pa traded honey and bush-meat.

It was small and had been fixed high up on a wall above the bar. But this TV was huge. The chief ran his hand along the top of the screen, thanking General Chan.

General Chan swung his arm in an arc across the bare ground where we were sitting. He waited until the camera was on him. 'The only thing missing is a school,' he said. 'This is where we will build one. Right here.'

I felt Ma squeeze my arm and I looked up at her. She nodded and smiled and I leant into her.

Maybe Grandfather was wrong. Maybe life could be better here. I could go to school. We wouldn't need rice handouts when we grew our own. We could see a doctor if we were sick. We didn't have electricity yet, but it would come. When it did, we would be able to study at night and Ma would be able to do her embroidery. Maybe we could even have a TV too.

We could live here.

This was our new village.

Our new life.

I wanted to tell Grandfather to come and live with us.

I wanted him to know life could be good.

CHAPTER 4

'Ow!' I rubbed my shoulder where a clod of earth had struck me.

'Hey, Tam! Look at you! You're fat and lazy now.'

I looked up and grinned. Noy was standing in front of me, silhouetted against the midday sun, his slingshot aimed at me. He let another clod of earth fly and it hit me on the cheek. I brushed it off and sat up. I must have dozed off in the heat. The smoke-haze from slash-and-burn farming in the hills hung like a grey fog between us and the sky. We hadn't seen the moon or stars since we'd arrived at our new village. It was much hotter here than our old home in the mountains. There was no cooling breeze, not even at night.

Noy loaded a small pebble in the slingshot. 'Too fat to fight, Tam?'

It was true. I'd filled out since we'd moved into our new homes. My ribs didn't stick out so much and the tops of my legs were now thicker than my knees. We'd all been given rice and General Chan had promised more. I'd eaten more rice since we'd moved than I'd eaten all year, even though Pa said we should be careful not to use it up too quickly. He said it would take a long time to grow our own.

Noy pelted me again. The pebble cracked against my skull. I scrambled up and he darted away, ducking behind the concrete posts holding our new house from the ground.

'Too slow,' he taunted.

I set off after him along the track. Chickens scattered in a flurry of dust and feathers in front of us. Dogs barked. Children shouted for Noy and then for me. The stilted houses passed in a blur. Noy ducked under a line of washed blankets and sprinted along the road out from the village. I ran after him, my feet flying across the dirt. I caught up with him at the village edge and pulled him down and we fell in a sprawling mass in the dirt, laughing and catching our breath. Dust-red rivers of sweat ran down his face. I grabbed a handful of grit and tried to shove it down Noy's shirt, but he pushed me away.

'Get off,' he scowled.

Moon Bear

I chucked another handful of earth and glared at him. He was always the one to decide the game was over. But Noy was already sitting up and looking beyond the low rise of scrubland to the highway in the distance. Dust-clouds followed two lorries rumbling southbound.

He turned to me, his head tilted to one side. 'Have you been to the Mekong yet, Tam?'

'No,' I said. I frowned at him. We both knew only some of the elders had been down to the river to buy fishing nets.

'Me neither,' said Noy.

Beyond the highway, hidden from view behind scrubland and fields lay the great Mekong. The River of all Rivers.

A slow smile spread across Noy's face.

It reminded me of the night he dared me to take the moon bear cub. I scooped some dirt and let it trickle through my fingers. The image of the cub had stayed with me. I was glad it was still free in the forest. I often thought about Grandfather too. I imagined him collecting wild honey from the bees and setting nets to fish the river. I imagined him sleeping beneath the stars we could not see.

Noy whacked my arm. 'Wake up, Tam!' He stood up and brushed the dirt from his clothes. 'Come on, let's go and see the Mekong for ourselves.'

I should have been still helping Pa, but I'd slipped away. My hands and fingers were sore and blistered from pulling stones and thick rooted weeds from the ground. I couldn't see Ma. She was probably with him too.

'I have to help in the fields,' I said.

Noy shrugged his shoulders and set off down the track. His heels kicked up puffs of red dust behind him. I thought he'd turn round to see if I was following, but he kept on walking, straight on. I glanced back at the village. We wouldn't be *that* long. If we hurried, we wouldn't even be missed. I wanted to see the Mekong. I'd heard stories about it, of fish as big as elephants and water dragons living deep beneath its surface. Most of all I didn't want Noy to see it before me.

'Wait,' I called after him. 'Wait.'

He didn't stop and I had to run to catch up with him.

He only stopped where our track met the main highway. It ran north and south, a long straight line of new tarmac. The road was empty except for a glint of metal in the far distance. I stepped out onto the road. The surface was tacky in the heat. It smelt of tar and tyre rubber. The heat burned into my soles and I had to leap across in long footsteps. Noy followed, wiping his feet in the dust on the far side to cool them down.

Moon Bear

The glint of metal in the distance was getting bigger. It shimmered in the heat haze, a ripple of red and black and silver. It was getting nearer all the time. The drone from its engines filled the air. A motorbike emerged, its rider tucked close as if he were part of the machine too. He lifted the front wheel off the ground, as he roared past, leaving us in a whirlwind of dust and puff of smoke. I looked across at Noy, but he stood open-mouthed watching it disappear into the distance.

'Did you see that?' he said. 'Did you see it?'

I rubbed the dust from my eyes and turned away. 'Come on. I thought you said we were going to the river.'

The Mekong was larger than I expected. It was wide and slow, dust yellow, like the earth. It was nothing like the fast rivers of the mountains that churned white and misted the air with spray. The Mekong was busy too. Long thin riverboats with open sides and tin roofs carried people and sacks, and animals of all sorts crammed in cages. The boats were travelling both ways up and down the river. On the far side, fishermen stood waist deep in the shallows casting nets out into the water. A buffalo lay submerged, only his nose and wide horns sticking above the water.

I climbed down to the smooth rocks at the water's edge. I guessed they were shaped by the Mekong in full monsoon flood. A scum of river froth and plastic clung in the still water trapped between the rocks.

I waded out knee deep, letting the cool water swirl around me.

Noy joined me. He dipped his head in the water and flung it back spraying water in an arc behind him. He wiped the dust from his face and pointed at the longboats heading downstream. 'Know where they're going?'

I shrugged my shoulders. 'Do you?'

Noy laughed. 'Don't you know anything, Tam? They're going to the *city*.' His eyes widened as he said this and drew out the word *city* slowly from his mouth.

I bent down and washed my face, scooping the water with both my hands. It tasted different to our mountain rivers too.

Noy waded further out. 'There's work in the city.'

I looked at him. His eyes were fixed downstream.

'We've got land to farm here,' I said.

Noy snorted. 'There's money in the city, Tam. That's what I'm talking about. Money.' He turned and grinned at me. 'We could go there. You and me. We'd get jobs there. We'd look out for each other.'

Moon Bear

I stared at him. Was he being serious or playing games?

'We couldn't leave the village,' I said.

Noy frowned, his face unreadable. 'Couldn't we?'

We stood in silence staring out across the river. How had I not noticed? The water wasn't still and calm at all. It churned beneath. Undercurrents boiled up from the depths, rising and swirling in spinning whirlpools and folding back under again, as if it was trying to hold its secrets deep inside.

Noy turned to face me. 'One day, Tam, I'm going to go. And no one can stop me. I'm going to walk out of here and go.'

'What about your family?'

Noy snorted. 'I'll come back. And when I do I'll be riding a motorbike like the one we saw today. Only it'll be my bike. Bought with my money. My father will be proud of me. It will be me he turns to, not my brother. Maybe he will make me the chief.'

I watched him turn and walk away, kicking his feet against clumps of river grass that grew between the rocks. Noy and I had grown up together. We'd hunted together with our slingshots in the forest, caught our first fish from the fast river. We'd grown up like brothers. Yet, as I looked at him, I didn't feel I knew him now at all. Maybe one of his souls had strayed too far and couldn't find its way back. Maybe one of his souls had already joined the Mekong and been drawn into its current, already on its way towards the city.

CHAPTER 5

Maybe it was because another full moon had passed since we had moved from our old village, but it began to really feel as if this could be our home here. The chickens had settled into their new roosts and we didn't need to corral the pigs to stop them wandering any more. Ma had traded flower-cloths on the highway for lamp oil and new nets to fish the Mekong. I'd killed six white-bellied rats for the pot with my slingshot. Ma was pleased, as we couldn't hunt bush meat from the forest. Our old life in the mountains became like a distant memory. It didn't seem real any more, more like part of a dream.

Mae and Sulee had been for lessons with the new teacher who came to teach in the shade beneath the spreading branches of the flame tree. I didn't go with them. I had to help Pa in the fields, to clear the weeds and stones and dig the irrigation channels for the rice. We didn't have much time before the rains came.

I slung the pick and shovel across my back and headed out to the fields. My feet scuffed the hot earth. My mouth felt dry. Everything felt dry. I imagined the throat of the earth waiting for the rain. I imagined rain pitting the dust, filling up the cracks and ditches and streambeds. It wouldn't be long. The monsoon was coming. I could feel it. The dust in the air sparkled with it. One day soon, the rains would come.

I passed other villagers bent double, their wide-brimmed hats keeping off the sun. Our field was the furthest away, set back into the corner of a low hill. Pa had worked hard to clear the stones although we'd have to wait for the rains to soften the earth before we could plough and level it. He said we would plant fruit trees on the hill. Maybe even keep some bees. Not the wild ones, like in the forest, but we'd keep them in wooden hives. Pa understood bees. They understood him too.

I found him marking out the irrigation channel along the border of our field. In the monsoon, we would rely on water from the hills, but General Chan had promised us a water pump for dry season. It meant we would be able to grow other crops all year too.

Moon Bear

Pa straightened up, pushing his hand into the small of his back. 'We need the handcart too, Tam. We have to move these stones.'

I laid the pick and shovel on the ground next to him. 'I'll get it now.'

Pa wiped the sweat from his face. 'And a drink, Tam. Bring water when you come back.'

I ran along our field edge and only stopped when I reached the low rise of the hill. I turned back to look at Pa. He was stooped to reach the pickaxe. He looked out of place here. In our old village, my father was the Bee Man. He walked tall in the forests. He talked to the bees. The bees told him everything. But here, without the forest, my father was just a farmer, just a man.

Sunlight flashed on the pickaxe as he swung it high above his head.

Maybe if the forest bees had been here, they could have warned him. Maybe the bees would have seen the rusted metal casing hidden untouched beneath forty years of mud and weeds.

But there were no forest bees.

I watched the pick swing in a slow arc and sink into the ground.

There was no warning.

None.
The ground exploded and lifted up into the sky.
Mud and earth and stone rained down.
And when the dust cleared,
my father
the Bee Man,
was gone.

CHAPTER 6

'**B**ombies!'

A man from the bomb clearance team held up a poster of a long metal tube filled with fist sized metal balls.

'Cluster bombs,' he said.

The men in the van, with their padded jackets and metal detectors, had arrived the day after Pa was killed. One was foreign, a *falang*. He was a big man with yellow hair. His white skin was reddened on his face and forearms. He had a huge nose like an overripe tomato. The other men were from Laos, from the city. They had scanned the earth with their metal detectors, working slowly up and down the fields. Six bombs were found in our field alone and two in the centre of the village. They told Ma it was lucky that I hadn't been killed too. But it should have been me. It would have been better if it had been me. I wonder if Ma thought that too. Who would work the fields now Pa was gone? Where would we live now there was no man to head our household?

'Bombies,' the man said again.

Everyone from the village was crowded into the chief's hut. Children sat on the floor and adults stood in a ring around the sides. Even General Chan was here with two of his men in suits. They had arrived in his helicopter spinning dust into the sky. I noticed he didn't have his cameraman with him today. Noy said he'd heard the General wasn't pleased about the bomb. Other villagers might hear about it and not want to leave the mountains.

I sat near the back with Ma and my sisters. It was hot and airless in the room. Mae buried her head into my chest. She hadn't spoken since Pa died. Sulee gripped my arm. I could feel her fingers dig into my skin.

The man held up another poster, of bombs falling from a plane. 'Three hundred million of these were dropped on Laos between 1964 and 1973. A planeload of bombs every eight minutes, every hour, twenty-four hours a day.' He spoke the figures slowly then paused and looked around.

The room was silent. I glanced at Ma, but she was staring into space as if her mind was far, far away.

The man tapped his hand against the poster. 'Our country has been the most heavily bombed country in the history of the world. Ever.' He said this with a strange mix of awe and national pride. He leant forward and lowered his voice. 'It was the American's secret war.'

How could so many bombs be kept secret? I knew Grandfather fought as a boy soldier in that war, but he'd never spoken about it. The only sign was the long scar on his leg. Maybe it was his secret war too.

The man held up another poster of a bomb hidden beneath grass and weeds. 'Many bombs exploded when they hit the ground, but many didn't. Millions lie unexploded in our villages and fields.'

I stared at the picture. My head felt light and white. A bomb like this had waited for more than forty years to tear Pa's souls apart. The man's voice became muffled and sounded far away.

I got up and pushed past Ma. 'I need some air.'

I started walking out of the village. I didn't know where. I wanted to run and run. I had a crazy idea I could get to the mountains. Somehow start over again with Grandfather in the forests, like it used to be. Above, the sky had darkened. It glowed with the deep blue monsoon light. Cloud bellies swelled with rain. I could taste the water in the air. The distant ridge of mountains had merged into a haze of blue. On the mountains it was raining already.

'Hey, Tam!'

I turned.

Noy was running to catch up with me. 'Where're you going?'

I slumped down on the ground and waited for him. I dug my fingers in the dry earth. There was nowhere to run to. 'I don't know,' I said.

Noy crouched next to me and picked up a handful of dirt, letting it run through his fingers. I could see him watching me. 'Rain's coming,' he said.

I nodded.

Our field lay empty. The deep crater left by the bomb had been filled in. The irrigation ditches lay half dug. It wasn't ready for the rice.

I looked at Noy. 'What will I do? What will I do now Pa's gone?'

Noy picked up another handful and let it slip through his fingers. Around us, big dark spots of rain began to pit the hot ground, sending little puffs of steam into the air. He held out his palm to catch the rain.

'What will I do?' I said.

Moon Bear

He got up and brushed the dust from his knees. 'Come on, let's get back.'

By the time we reached the village, we were soaked. The clouds had opened and rain hammered on the tin roofs and fell in sheets of water to the ground. It pooled beneath the houses and cut channels through the soft earth, running in red rivers along tyre tracks in the road. The chickens had been flushed out from their roosts in the dirt hollows and they huddled together on raised patches of dry earth, their feathers fluffed and their heads tucked beneath their wings.

I followed Noy back to his house. The villagers had left. Only Noy's family was there with General Chan and the men from the bomb clearance team. Ma was there too. They all turned when I walked through the door. Tomato-nose man put his hand on my shoulder and smiled at me. He spoke words I didn't understand.

'He says he is sorry about your father,' said one man from the bomb team. 'But he is very happy that the General will help your family.'

I glanced at General Chan. He was sitting on a low stool, sipping his tea. His eyes were fixed on Tomato-nose.

'Tam.' The chief walked over to me. Everyone was looking my way. Noy took a step back to let him pass.

The chief cleared his throat. 'Tam, you are the man in your family now. You must help your mother, now your father is no longer here.'

'Of course,' I said.

Ma wouldn't look at me.

The chief glanced at Ma and then at me. 'But you are not old enough to take on the land. You are a boy still.'

I looked at Ma and Sulee and Mae. What would become of them if I didn't work?

'I can,' I said. 'I will. I'll work hard. I will plant our rice.'

The chief put his hand on my shoulder. 'General Chan knows of a job in the city. It will pay well and you can send the money to your family. It may be the only way your mother can keep the house.'

I glanced at General Chan. He sat impassive, sipping his tea.

I lowered my voice. I hoped General Chan would not hear above the rain. 'I can dig the fields. I can plant the rice. I know I can.'

The chief frowned at me and raised his voice. 'Tam, I know you share our gratitude for General Chan. He wishes to help our village. He wishes to help you and your family. He has been kind enough to find you work on a farm in the city.'

Moon Bear

I looked around. Tomato-nose was smiling and nodding at me. Ma wouldn't catch my eye. Noy was glaring at
me, his face dark like the monsoon sky. Was he jealous? Did
he want to go to the city? He could have the city for all I
cared. I couldn't go. Ma needed me.

I needed her.

The chief was still looking at me. 'Any questions, Tam?'

The rain drummed harder on the roof, the sound
drumming against my skull. My mind was blank. Empty.
I stood in the centre of the room, water dripping from my
wet clothes, pooling at my feet.

'Then fetch your things,' he said. 'General Chan will
take you with him to the city today.'

My legs were heavy, as if they were stuck deep in
thick mud. I watched General Chan finish his tea and stand
up to leave.

How could I work on a farm in the city? I only knew
about chickens and pigs and hunting in the mountains.

'General Chan,' I said.

He turned to me, as if he had seen me for the first
time. The sides of his mouth curled downwards.

The chief shifted from one foot to the other, his face
strained. I knew I shouldn't have spoken directly to the
General.

The rain stopped as suddenly as it had started.

Water dripped from the gutters.

The ground outside hissed with the sound of steam rising from the hot earth.

'General Chan,' I said again. My voice was loud in the silence. 'What sort of farm is it?'

General Chan glanced at the chief and Ma. He wouldn't look at me. He pulled the sleeve of his jacket to look at the gold watch on his wrist. 'We must go,' he said.

He turned and left. His footsteps echoed hollowly in the room.

I stared after him.

Why didn't he answer?

My mind filled with that one question.

What *do* you farm in a city?

CHAPTER 7

Ma helped me pack up the few things I owned; my clothes, my slingshot, and Pa's new flip-flops, though they were too big for me still. She wrapped up a tin of forest honey in oilcloth. It was the last honey Pa and Grandfather had collected from the forests. It felt a lifetime ago, although only two months had passed. Yet now, I was moving on again.

There was no time for long goodbyes. Ma wrapped cotton around my wrists to keep my souls safe inside. She touched her palms against my face. 'Remember who you are,' she said. 'Keep safe, Tam, and come back to us.'

I put my hands on hers. I wanted to stay there in the darkness of our house. I wanted to stay with Ma and Sulee and Mae.

Outside, cars revved their engines. I heard the chief shout my name.

Sulee held on to me, but Ma pulled her hand away.

How could I leave?

Mae struggled to reach me, pushing her arms through Ma's grip. But Ma held her tight.

'Tam!' The chief called my name again.

I couldn't move. I stood, staring at Ma and Sulee and Mae clinging to each other. 'I should go,' I said.

Ma nodded. She blinked back tears and smiled. 'I will pray that Good Luck finds you.'

I took a deep breath, picked up my bag and left.

I turned once to see Ma watching me through the door of the house. Mae clung to her skirts and Sulee screamed my name. What if something happened to them? Who would tell me? How would I know?

'Tam!' The chief was standing beside the bomb clearance van. 'Come on. General Chan said these men will take you to the city.'

I looked around but General Chan's helicopter had gone. He and the men in suits had already left. The chief helped me into the back of the van where I wedged myself between metal detectors and sacks and shovels. Noy didn't show up to say goodbye. I could see him watching from the window of his house, his face half hidden in shadow. The chief slammed the van doors and plunged me into darkness. I felt the van lurch and slide along the track until we reached the highway. We picked up speed and I could hear the steady rush of air against the sides and the spray of water from the wheels on the wet road.

It was hot and airless in the van. A wire grille behind the driver's seat let a little light through. I could see the back of the heads of the bomb men and Tomato-nose.

A voice called through the grille. 'Are you all right back there?'

I shifted in my seat and tried to push away the shovels that dug into my back. 'Yes,' I grunted.

I hugged my bag of belongings against my chest. I could feel the tin of forest honey press against my skin. My stomach ached. I hadn't eaten all day. I unwrapped the oilcloth and ran my fingers around the rim. Just one taste, I told myself. I'd save the rest. I lifted the lid and scooped some honey, sucking the smoky bitter-sweetness from my fingers. I closed my eyes. I tasted the forest, the leaves and flowers. I tasted the damp earth where the bear cub had curled safe inside his den. I tasted Ma sewing her flower-cloths, and Mae and Sulee playing in the sun-bright pools below the waterfalls. I tasted Grandfather in his poppy field, calling

the bees, and Pa smiling from under his wide-brimmed hat.
I tasted all these things.

I sank my head onto my knees.

I was glad of the darkness.

I closed the tin lid and pressed it tight.

I promised myself I would never open it again.

Never.

I would never taste it.

I would never even try.

I was glad of the darkness, because in the darkness,
no one can see you cry.

CHAPTER 8

The bang of doors woke me. Light flooded the van. I sat up and rubbed my neck. It was stiff from lying crooked up against hard boxes. The driver helped me out and dropped my bag on the ground beside me.

I stood blinking in the late afternoon sunlight.

We were in a yard surrounded by high metal fencing, topped with a roll of barbed wire. Two logging trucks, like the ones I'd seen in the mountains, were parked up on the far side. One was hitched up on its side having a tyre changed. Cars with prices on their bonnets were lined up against the fence facing the road. They shone beetle-bright in the sunlight.

Beyond the fence, cars and motorbikes and tuk-tuks moved in a steady stream along a wide road. The air was filled with dust and noise. So much noise. So this is what it was like in the city.

A man in blue overalls was walking across the yard towards us.

'This is Mr Sone,' said the driver. 'He owns Sone Motors. He will take care of you now.'

Mr Sone stood in front of me. He was a tall man, taller than our chief. His hands were black with oil and he clutched a spanner in one of them. He looked me up and down, his eyes resting on my torn shirt and my bare feet. He turned to the driver. 'He looks young,' he said. 'We were expecting someone older.'

The driver shrugged his shoulders. 'General Chan said to bring him here.'

Mr Sone walked in a circle around me. 'How old are you, boy?'

I stared at the ground, watching Mr Sone's work boots come to a stop in front of me.

'What's your name?' he said.

I concentrated on my feet caked in a thick layer of dirt. 'Tam,' I said. 'My name is Tam.'

'Do you have family?'

I nodded.

Mr Sone turned to the driver. 'Then I think you

should take him back.'

The driver ran his hands through his hair. He leant in at the window of his van. I could see him talking to Tomato-nose. Tomato-nose took a swig of water from a bottle and wiped his face. I felt their eyes on me. I couldn't go back, however much I wanted to. I had to earn money for Ma. It was the only way she could keep the house we'd been given. She was relying on me.

I picked my bag from the ground and slung it across my shoulder, trying to look more confident than I felt. 'I am here to work,' I said.

Mr Sone exchanged glances with the driver. The driver shrugged his shoulders and said something I couldn't hear. I watched him climb into the car and rev the engine. Tomato-nose gave a thumbs-up and a cheery wave as they drove away in a swirl of exhaust and dust.

Mr Sone watched them go and then turned to me. 'Follow me,' he grunted.

I walked close behind him across the yard into the darkness of a garage and almost tripped on a pair of legs sticking out from under a car.

'My eldest son, Rami,' said Mr Sone, striding ahead. 'He works for me.'

I glanced back but could only hear the clink of metal

on metal from underneath the car.

I had to run to keep up with Mr Sone. At the far end of the garage he turned and slipped through a low doorway to a house next to the entrance to the yard. The smells of cooking rice and spices filtered through the open window. Mr Sone kicked off his boots and walked through the door.

He put his hand out. 'Wait there. I will call my wife.'

Inside, I could see big pans steaming on a cooker in the corner. A boy my age sat at a table with books spread out in front of him. He rolled a pencil around his fingers and stared at me.

'Kee,' shouted Mr Sone. 'We have our lodger.'

A small woman came through a door on the far side. She wiped her hands on her apron and looked at me. 'He looks young.'

Mr Sone washed his hands in the sink, working soap along his forearms. 'He's from the mountains,' he said.

The boy at the table put down his pencil. 'He stinks,' he said.

'That's enough, Kham,' snapped Mrs Sone. She stepped closer to me and wrinkled her nose. 'Are you hungry?'

I nodded.

Moon Bear

She set a bowl and spoon on the table. 'Eat first, then we will show you your room and the shower.'

Kham stared at me as his mother ladled noodle soup into a bowl.

I was so hungry that I ate one whole bowl and when Mrs Sone offered another, I ate that too.

Mrs Sone frowned and looked at her husband. 'We'll have to charge more if he always eats this much.'

I stopped eating and put my spoon back on the table. 'I have no money to pay you,' I said.

Mr Sone looked across at me. 'The Doctor is paying your rent.'

'The Doctor?' I said. 'Who's he?'

Mr and Mrs Sone exchanged glances.

Mr Sone took a sip of water and cleared his throat. 'The Doctor is the owner of the farm. You will be working for him. He will pay me your rent before he sends the rest of your earnings to your family.'

I clasped my hands beneath the table. 'Where is the Doctor's farm? How long will it take to get there?'

Kham snorted a laugh. 'Don't you *know*?'

Mrs Sone rapped her spoon down on the table. 'Kham, eat up. It's nearly bedtime for you. You have school in the morning.'

Mrs Sone led me outside to a corrugated iron shed beside the garage. She pushed open the door. 'This is your room,' she said. The shed was dark, but smelt clean inside. A shaft of light cut through a high window on the far wall. She pulled a cord and lit the room from a bare light bulb on the ceiling. The room was empty except for a mattress, a small cupboard and a table in the corner. She pressed a towel into my hands. 'You can use the shower Mr Sone's workers use.'

I stood there, clutching the towel in my hands.

Mrs Sone put her hand on her hip. 'Any questions?'

'Where can I find the Doctor?

Mrs Sone turned to leave. 'The Doctor will come for you in the morning,' she said. Her face softened and she put her hand on my arm. 'Make sure you are ready for him.'

I closed the door and listened to her footsteps fade away. My room was small, but at least it was my space for now. I had a place to eat and sleep and a job with the Doctor who would send my money back home. I pulled the light cord. Off. On. Off. On. A moth batted around the light bulb. I tried to imagine our house in the village with electricity. I imagined it lit up like the city. I pulled the cord again and stood in the darkness. Outside, the sky had darkened. The orange haze of streetlight filtered through the high window. I listened to the sounds of the city night. Car horns. A siren. Tuk-tuks and motorbikes buzzing along the road outside. Music pumping from a car. Shouts and laughter.

I pushed the table beneath the high window and climbed up to look outside. I could see Mr Sone talking to a lorry driver beneath the floodlights of the garage yard. Beyond the road and the dust screen from the traffic, lay a long low concrete building. It was windowless, except for narrow openings just beneath the flat iron roof. Next to the building, tall metal gates were firmly closed and locked with a thick chain and padlock. In the evening light I strained my eyes to make out the image painted on the gates. It looked like a bear, a moon bear, but it seemed so strange to see it here. Somewhere inside the building, a hard white light flickered, making the darkness seem a deeper dark.

I shivered.

Beyond that building were more buildings, going on and on. Nowhere could I see any green. Not even a scrubby patch of grass.

'Tam!'

The light flicked on. I spun round to see Kham holding up a clean T-shirt and shorts.

'Ma said you're to have these,' he said. He laid them on the mattress and climbed up next to me. 'What are you looking at?'

I pointed to the concrete building. 'What's that?'

'Didn't anyone tell you?' Kham stared across the road. 'That's the Doctor's farm.'

My mouth felt dry. 'What sort of farm?' I said.

Kham took his time to answer.

'Tam,' he said. 'Have you ever seen a bear?'

CHAPTER 9

I woke to loud banging. I tried to push the sleep from my head and remember where I was. The noise. The traffic. A pale light slanted through the window grilles. It was morning already.

Still the banging. Thump, thump, thump.

I sat bolt upright and spun round to look behind me. The banging was coming from my room. A man was standing in the doorway, thumping his fist against the door frame. He was small and wiry, wearing skinny jeans and a tight white T-shirt. His sunglasses sat perched on his slicked back hair. His right leg jiggled and he chewed gum as he spoke. 'Well, Mountain Boy, first day at work and you're late.'

I stared at him.

He threw a pair of gumboots. They bounced on the ground and skidded to a halt against the mattress. The soles were worn and the rubber had split along the heel on one boot. 'You'll need these for the job. I'll take them from your first week's pay.' He spat out his chewing gum. 'If you don't get a move on, I'll dock a day's pay too.'

I scrambled to my feet. So this was the Doctor. I thought of Ma and the money she needed me to earn. How could I have slept in, on my first day? I pulled on a top and shorts and slid my feet in the gumboots. They were much too big. My feet slipped around inside. Maybe they were the last worker's boots. I wondered what had happened to him.

I pulled the blanket straight on my bed and faced the Doctor. 'I'm ready.'

The Doctor gave a short laugh. He smiled, showing a gold tooth in the corner of his mouth. 'Really?' He leant close. 'No one is ever ready for the bears.'

I closed the door of my room and followed the Doctor out onto the street. The sun had not long been up. It hovered above the rooftops, a pale yellow ball, veiled by dust and smog. The city was awake already. Tuk-tuks and cars filled the road. A line of shaven-headed monks walked along the pavement, their saffron robes bright against the paler yellow of the early morning sky. I watched them pass. Some were boys not much older than me. They bowed to collect the offerings of rice from women kneeling on the floor. I saw Kham's mother with them. She placed sticky rice into their bowls. My stomach ached with hunger. I guessed I'd have no food until later on in the day.

'Hey, Mountain Boy, come on.'

I turned and stepped out onto the road. A truck's horn blasted in my ear and I felt the Doctor's fingers dig into my arm and pull me back. The truck's wing mirror flicked against my shoulder.

The Doctor glared at me. 'Careful, Mountain Boy. You don't want to get killed on the road.' He caught me by the elbow and half pushed and half dragged me through the traffic. He pushed open the tall red gates of the bear farm. 'We'll let the bears do that instead.'

Beyond the high metal gates was a bare dirt yard surrounded by walls. Bags of rubbish, pooled in dirty water, were heaped up in a corner. A bicycle was propped up against one wall and a motorbike stood in the only patch of clean

concrete. A small office room was set against the low concrete building. Sliding metal doors to the building were
firmly shut. It was strangely quiet in there too. Dead quiet.

Through the office window, I could see a man
slumped in the chair, a beer bottle resting on his belly. His
head was tipped back and his mouth lay open. He was half
hidden behind a fug of cigarette smoke.

'This way,' said the Doctor. He kicked the door
open and the man shot up in his seat. His beer bottle fell
onto the floor. It bounced and spun spreading a circle trail
of beer. The man picked up some papers on the table and
shuffled them.

'Asang!' The Doctor picked up the bottle and thumped
it on the table. 'I have found you another assistant.'

Asang wiped his mouth and glanced between the
Doctor and me. His belly bulged through his shirt, between
the gaps left by missing buttons. A spiral of smoke drifted
upwards from his cigarette.

The Doctor gave me a shove. 'Mountain Boy. This is
Asang. Asang tells you what to do. And I tell Asang what
to do. Is that clear?'

I nodded.

The Doctor picked up a sheaf of papers and flicked
through them. Beads of sweat ran down Asang's face. It was

hot and stuffy in the office. A broken fan hung from the ceiling. Piles of papers were stacked on a filing cabinet in the corner of the room and the tabletop was littered with pens and cigarette ends. The shelves above Asang's head were lined with small glass bottles. Some bottles were empty, yet others were filled with a dark brown sludge. There were clear plastic envelopes containing white pills and powders, labelled with words I couldn't read. Each label bore the picture of a black bear standing on its hind legs, a white crescent on its chest.

'Come,' said the Doctor. 'It's time our Mountain Boy did some work.'

The Doctor took off his trainers and slipped his feet into a pair of gumboots. On the way out, he picked up a long metal bar from behind the door. As he gripped the metal, I noticed how clean and smooth his hand was, not a farmer's hand at all.

Asang followed, slopping along in rubber shoes. We stopped at the low concrete building. Asang hauled on the sliding doors and they rolled open, metal grating on the concrete. I could hear movements from inside the building, but it was too dark to see. The only light came from the window grilles high up on the walls. It cut in blades across the roof space high above our heads.

I covered my face as the stench filled my nose and mouth.

The Doctor turned to me. 'Bears stink,' he said. 'Get used to it.'

The air from the building stank of dirt and dead things. It was nothing like the clean earthy smell of the bear den.

The building had fallen silent again, as if whatever was inside was waiting for us.

The Doctor stepped in and reached up beside the door. Somewhere deep inside, a white light flickered and buzzed into life. Three strips of neon lit up in a row high above the centre of the building.

The Doctor swept his arm inside. 'Welcome to the bear barn,' he said, and looked right at me. 'It is time we introduced you to my bears.'

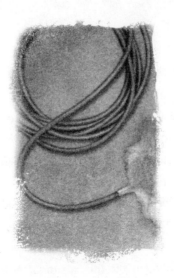

CHAPTER 10

I didn't know what to expect. Maybe I thought I'd see bears running freely in the building. But in the harsh glare of the neon strip-lights there were eight cages, set in two rows either side of a long central drainage channel. The cages were held up from the ground on metal posts fixed into the concrete. Beneath each cage the concrete was crusted in bear filth. Trails of brownish liquid ran towards the drainage gutter.

The Doctor put his hands on his hips. 'These are all my bears,' he said. 'Come, Mountain Boy. Come and see.'

I couldn't move. I just stared. They didn't look like bears at first. They were huge black shapes, filling up the space inside each cage. Some lay, their paws dangling through the bars. Others sat, swaying from side to side. I could see they were moon bears from the crescents of white fur on their chests.

'Come, Mountain Boy,' said the Doctor. He pulled my arm. 'Don't tell me you're scared.'

I walked behind him along the row. He ran his metal bar along the metal of the cage fronts. The noise rang out inside the building. The bears became restless. They hooted and moaned and moved to the far side of their cages, pressing themselves against the bars. They were so big, so close, so real. I never knew bears could be kept like this. What did the Doctor keep them *for*?

I followed the Doctor to an end cage. Inside was a huge bear, much bigger than any of the others. Unlike the other bears, this bear didn't cower when the Doctor approached. It faced him, its head pressed against the bars. The Doctor slammed his metal bar against the cage and the bear exploded, snarling and lashing out with its paws.

I shot backwards.

The Doctor laughed. 'This is Biter. My first bear.' He held up his left hand and I noticed for the first time that two of the Doctor's fingers were missing. The Doctor pulled something from under the neckline of his T-shirt. Bear teeth were threaded on a strip of leather around his neck. The Doctor leant close. 'He took my fingers. So I took his teeth.' He struck Biter in the belly with the metal bar. 'We have an understanding, don't we, bear?'

Biter lashed out and bit at the cage bars. I could see the line of broken teeth along his jaw. The bear pushed its paw through the bars. His long claws slashed the air. I backed away into another cage where the bear inside groaned and pressed itself against the furthest bars.

'And that one's Mama Bear,' said the Doctor, banging his bar against her cage. 'She was pregnant when we got her. That's her cub over there.'

Mama Bear flattened her ears and moaned. She rolled her eyes, the whites showing. Her mouth hung open. She panted in the heat. Her cub in the next cage was a full-grown bear. He swung his head from side to side, hitting his head against the bars each time.

'Dumb bear does that all day,' said the Doctor. 'Only stops swinging his head when he eats.'

The Doctor scraped at the dried bear mess on the concrete with his gumboots and wrinkled his nose. He took the wire yard brush from Asang and pushed it into my hands. 'Your job is to clean these floors. Make sure you do a better job than the last worker here.'

I watched the Doctor walk away, banging his metal bar against the cages. He paused at the sliding doors and spun round. 'Asang,' he shouted. 'I will be back to-morrow. We will show Mountain Boy how we milk the bears.'

I heard the motorbike rev up in the compound and could see the Doctor ride out through the red gates. The bears seemed to relax and shuffle in their cages.

'This way,' said Asang. It was the first time I'd heard him speak. He pointed to the yard brushes and a coiled hose. 'Come and find me when you're done.'

I watched him walk away to the office. Despite the heat, Asang closed the door, and soon a fog of cigarette smoke screened the office from view.

I stared along the line of bears. Could I really work here? What if the bears escaped? Biter looked as though he wanted to tear me apart. I started working around the cages at first. I didn't want to get in paws' reach of the bears. I hosed and scraped the concrete floor. The dirt below the cages was so dry and crusted that I had to let the water soak through to soften it. My arms ached and I was pouring with sweat, but I thought of Ma. I wanted to make the Doctor pleased. I wanted to show that I could do this job. I wanted to make sure Ma received the money.

Moon Bear

As the day's heat rose outside, so did the heat inside. I could feel the sun's rays press down from the iron roof above. I drank from the hosepipe and sprayed myself with water. I couldn't see any water in the cages so I put my finger in the end of the hose and sprayed the bears too. They seemed to enjoy it, letting the cool water soak through their thick fur and run off onto the ground below. They rolled in their cramped cages and licked the water from their paws and fur.

I noticed that the front paw of some bears was missing. The leg ended in a stump. I thought of the snare traps Noy and I set for forest game. We'd caught a mousedeer once. Where the wire had caught its leg, the flesh was skinned and black by the time we'd found it. We'd killed it quickly and felt bad that we'd let it suffer. I wondered if the bears had been caught in snare traps too.

I didn't go near Biter. I sprayed him with water, but he shook it off staring at me all the time. I had to crouch low to scrape the dirt beneath his cage, watching him and keeping out of reach, in case he swung a paw down low.

I'd worked hard all day. I worked until I heard Asang's footsteps behind me. He looked around the building and scuffed the floor at some invisible piece of dirt. Steam rose from the wet bears and the washed floors.

'OK,' he said. 'We are done here for the day.' He reached up for the light switch and the building flickered into darkness.

I propped the brushes and scrapers back against the walls. 'Do we feed them too?'

Asang dropped his cigarette on the floor and crushed it with his heel. 'Not today. We don't feed them the day before we milk them. It is better that way.'

Asang pulled the sliding gates of the bear barn across. 'Go on, go,' he said. He closed the sliding doors, took his bicycle from the wall and ushered me out, locking the metal gates behind us. I watched him cycle down the road and become lost among the traffic.

The sun had arced across the sky and was sinking towards the rooftops. The day was still hot. Heat hung in the air, trapped below the city smog. My head felt light. All I wanted was to eat and lie down in my room.

On the far side of the road, I could see Kham with two other boys his age. They leant against the wire fence of his father's yard, watching me. I stepped out onto the road. The traffic didn't stop. It was a steady stream, most of the cars moving out of the city. I took a chance and dashed between the traffic. A motorbike had to swerve to miss me. Kham shook his head and the other two boys slapped him on the back and laughed. They held out their hands, while Kham put coins into their palms. I walked head down past them.

'Hey, Tam!'

I turned round.

Kham was running to catch up with me. 'How was it today?'

'It was OK,' I said.

'Did you see the bears?'

I kept walking to my room. 'Yes,' I said.

'What are they like?'

'Big,' I said. I put my hand out to open the door to my room, but Kham stepped in front of me.

He glanced back to his house and lowered his voice. 'You know the last worker was killed by a bear?'

I stared at him.

'Mauled to death,' he said. 'That's why you got the job.'

I kicked off my gumboots and paired them together by the door.

'Are you going to stay? Are you really going to work there?' said Kham.

I reached out for the handle. 'What else can I do?'

I left Kham standing in the doorway and stepped inside my room. A bowl of rice and fish and a plate of fruit were laid out on the table. My clothes had been washed and dried and a clean towel hung on a nail behind the door.

I took the towel. I wanted to wash to take the smell of sweat and bear away.

Kham was watching me from the doorway. 'I saw one once,' he said. 'Some loggers brought one on their lorry. They'd bound it up but it still managed to get free. It was one crazy bear. It was a good thing the yard gates were closed. We had to stay inside until the Doctor managed to sedate it. Ma said she didn't want any more bears coming to the yard. She says it's bad enough knowing they are so near.'

'They're locked up,' I said.

Kham leant into me. 'Then tell me,' he said, 'just how the last bear got out?'

From across the yard I could hear Kham's mother calling.

'Your ma wants you,' I said.

Kham reached inside his pocket. 'Maybe you would like to buy a small flashlight from me. Maybe you need one in the night?'

Moon Bear

I looked down at the three flashlights Kham had pulled out.

'Brand new,' said Kham. 'They all have new batteries.'

'I have no money,' I said.

'Well, maybe you could take one and pay me back.'

I shook my head. 'The money I earn is sent to my ma.'

Kham's mother called again.

Kham shrugged his shoulders. 'Ah well. It's your loss.'

I watched him walk back to his house and sit with his family around the table.

I stepped into the shower and turned the water on full. I let the water run across me and soak deep into my hair. Maybe I should open the door and walk away. I could keep on walking through the city and somehow find my way back home. But it was an impossible dream. I was just as trapped here as the bears. I stretched out my arms to touch the walls of the shower room. Maybe this is how the bears felt, caged and far from their homes. Maybe they were just as scared too.

I thought about tomorrow and what the Doctor had said. He said we'd milk the bears. I'd milked the chief's buffalo when we lived back in the mountains. I'd filled a pot with rich frothy milk for an orphan calf. But buffalos were gentle creatures.

How, I wondered, do you milk a bear?

CHAPTER 11

'U . . . D . . . C . . . A. Urso . . . deoxy . . . cholic . . . acid.' The Doctor lifted up a small glass bottle to the light and swirled a dark greenish liquid around inside. It clung to the sides of the bottle in a thick sludge. 'This is what we milk from the bears. Liquid money.' He smiled showing his gold tooth. 'Bear bile to you.'

I rested the yard brush against the wall and wiped sweat from my forehead. I'd been up early, waiting for Asang to open the red gates at first light. I'd cleaned and scrubbed beneath all the cages and swept the yard before the Doctor had arrived.

I squinted at the bottle he held in his hand. 'Bear bile?'

The Doctor pushed his fingers into my stomach, right up underneath my ribs. 'It comes from here, from the gall bladder. Do you know what I'm talking about, Mountain Boy?'

I took a step back and nodded. I'd seen the gall bladders of the pigs at slaughter. I'd seen the small round sacks near the liver, filled with greenish liquid. But I couldn't think how to get bile from a bear.

'Asang!' the Doctor shouted. 'It's time we milked our first bear.'

I watched Asang wheel a large trolley into the building. The bears became restless. They turned in their cages, pressing against the far bars. I could see the whites of their eyes. Some panted and made deep hooting sounds. I could feel my own heart thumping deep inside my chest. I could feel their fear too.

The Doctor slammed his metal bar against the cage. 'We'll start with this one.' The bear shrieked inside, its ears flat against its head, its lips pulled back showing a line of broken teeth. Asang snared the bear with a rope on a pole while the Doctor drew a syringe of clear liquid from a vial and injected it into the flank of the bear.

'There,' said the Doctor. 'And now we wait for him to sleep.'

I watched the bear. For a while he stared back at us, then his head began to droop. He stared at the floor, saliva dripping from his mouth. He began to sway and his front legs trembled.

The Doctor lit a cigarette and breathed deeply, filling his lungs. He puffed the pale grey smoke into the air. 'What do you know about bear farming, boy?'

I watched the bear sink onto his forepaws.

The Doctor leant closer, his face next to mine. I could smell the smoke around his mouth. 'He doesn't know much, does he, Asang? Maybe they don't teach them anything in the mountains.'

The bear's hind legs began to buckle.

The Doctor paced around his cage. 'In China there are farms with two thousand bears. Imagine that, Mountain Boy.' He took another puff on his cigarette. 'One day, *I* will have two thousand bears. I had forty bears on my farm in Vietnam before it was closed down. They don't like bile farming there any more. It is so much easier here, in Laos.' He rubbed invisible money between his fingers. 'It's easier to bend the rules.'

The bear's back legs gave way and he collapsed on the cage floor, his neck crooked against the corner. Asang poked him with the end of his pole, and when he didn't move, Asang opened the cage door and hauled the bear out onto the trolley.

Moon Bear

Asang pushed the trolley, and I followed him and the Doctor to a small room beside the office. I hadn't noticed the room before. It was windowless. A small sink stood in one corner. A table with a machine that looked like a tiny TV screen was pushed against the wall. There were flasks and bottles and tubes scattered on the table. The table had green stains and was crusted with dirt. Asang brought the trolley next to it, and pulled the bear onto its back, tying its legs to the four corners of the trolley.

The Doctor switched on the screen and a fuzzy black and white image appeared. 'This is an ultrasound machine,' he said. 'And this is the probe.' He held up a round plastic end of a long lead attached to the machine. 'It lets me see inside the bear.'

I stared at the screen while the Doctor smeared a clear jelly onto the probe. He ran it across the bear's belly. The picture on the screen broke up into patterns of white and black.

'This is the liver,' said the Doctor, pointing to white fuzz on the screen. 'And this,' he said, pointing to a round black circle in the centre, 'is the gall bladder.'

Asang handed him a long needle and I watched the Doctor pierce the skin.

The bear twitched. He grunted. I noticed he licked his lips. I couldn't help think he was feeling all this, even though he couldn't move. The Doctor guided the needle, and I watched the white line of the needle on the screen enter the gall bladder. The Doctor pushed a fine metal wire along the needle and pulled it out and licked the end. He nodded with satisfaction. 'Bear bile.'

Asang attached a long clear tube to the needle and to a pump and watched the sludgy liquid trail up the tube and drip into a glass bottle on the table.

The Doctor leant back in his chair. 'In China they don't use the ultrasound machines,' he said. 'They make a hole in the belly and let the bile drip out. But I use the ultrasound because I am a real doctor.' He looked at me and then at Asang. 'You have to be very clever to be a doctor. Isn't that right, Asang?'

Asang shuffled his feet and nodded.

The Doctor swirled the bottle as if it would encourage more bile to flow. 'So I know all about bear bile. It's good for you. It cures all ills. Sore throat, headaches, sores, bruising, cancer. Maybe even death.' He laughed and looked across at Asang. 'Some men think it helps them find a wife.'

Asang pulled his shirt down across his stomach.

When all the bile had drained, the Doctor pulled the needle from the bear and poured the bile into several small bottles. He swilled the sludge at the base with water and swigged it back, finishing it in one gulp. He pulled a bitter face and slammed the bottle on the table.

'Funny thing is,' he said. A smirk rose on one side of his mouth. 'There's no need to take bile from these bears. UCDA can be made in laboratories. But I don't tell my customers that. Besides, they wouldn't want to know. They think it's more potent if it's from a real bear.'

The Doctor milked four bears that day. When he'd finished, Asang gave me the mix of rice and water to feed them all. I slid the metal trays into their cages and they pushed their noses in, slurping up the food as if they hadn't seen food for weeks.

Only Mama Bear didn't eat. She lay hunched on the bars of her cage. Her eyes were dull and sunken, and she grunted at the end of every breath. Her fur was matted and stuck in clumps on her skin. She was watching me, following my every move. I stepped closer and crouched beside her. My face was so close to hers, only the cage bars between us. She was a wild animal, but when she looked at me with her dark eyes, it was as if she could see right into me. I felt as if she let me see inside her too, beyond her pain, into the forests and mountains that held her soul. She pushed a paw through the bars towards my hand, the toes on her paw outstretched. I reached out and touched the hard cracked soles of her feet, working my fingers into the soft fur between the pads. She gently squeezed my small fingers in her huge paw.

I couldn't look at her.

I closed my eyes and turned away.

'Mountain Boy!'

The Doctor was watching me. 'This isn't a petting zoo. I don't pay you to cuddle the bears.'

'I'm sorry,' I said. 'But this bear is sick.'

The Doctor peered in at Mama Bear. He spat on the ground. 'She is lazy. One thing I don't like is a lazy worker. Make sure you are here tomorrow and I will show you how we dry out the bile to make pills and powders.'

I watched the Doctor drive from the yard. Asang ushered me out and locked the gates. He turned and handed me the keys. 'Open up tomorrow and make sure you clean the bears before I arrive.'

I took the keys and slipped them around my neck. Asang swung his leg across his bike and pedalled away into the slow line of traffic. Across the road, I could see Kham and his friends. They stood, backs leaning on the wire

Moon Bear

fence, their hands pushed deep inside their pockets. They were pretending to be talking but they were watching me like hawks.

I couldn't care what they thought of me. I ignored them and stepped between the parked cars, out onto the road. My mind was filled with the image of Mama Bear.

I didn't see the motorbike. It slammed into my side. Time slowed down. I saw the shocked face of the motorcyclist through the visor of his helmet as he tried to keep control. I saw the world spin and spin and spin as I bounced across the bonnets of the cars, and the blackness of the tarmac as the road flew up to meet me.

CHAPTER 12

'Tam! Tam! Can you hear me?'

I opened my eyes. I focused on the bare light bulb above me. I could feel the mattress beneath me press against my back and legs. My whole body ached. I curled my fingers in my palms and breathed in slowly. It even hurt to breathe.

Kham's ma peered over and looked at me. 'Tam, are you OK?'

I nodded and tried to sit up, but she put her hand on my chest to keep me down. 'Don't move,' she said. She turned round. 'Kham, stay with him while I fetch some water to clean his wounds.'

I turned my head to look at Kham. He was staring at me, eyes wide. 'Ma says you're lucky to be alive.'

Moon Bear

I stretched my arms and then each leg, one at a time. I couldn't feel any broken bones.

Kham glanced back over his shoulder towards the open door. He leant forward and whispered, 'I owe you, though!'

I pushed myself to sit up. My head ached and I could see cuts across my knees where road grit had been pushed deep into the skin, but otherwise I seemed to be all right. 'What d'you mean?' I said.

Kham held up a fist of money in his hand. 'I bet my friends you'd be knocked over on the road within the week.'

I blinked and stared at him. 'Would you have got more if I'd been killed?'

Kham's eyes widened. 'I hadn't thought of that.' He broke into a grin. 'See! You are a better businessman than me.'

I touched my fingers to my head. A huge sore lump had swollen across my forehead.

Kham slapped me on the shoulder and I winced. 'No hard feelings,' he said. He reached into his pocket and pulled out a small red torch. 'Have this. Think of it as a thank you, from me.'

I took the torch from him and switched it on and off. 'Thank you,' I said, although I wasn't sure exactly what I was thanking him for.

Kham's ma glanced suspiciously at the torch when she came back in.

'It's a present,' said Kham. 'A get well present from me.'

Kham's ma narrowed her eyes at him. 'Get washed before supper,' she said.

I sat still while she bathed my cuts and made me drink her sweet, spiced tea. She finished and wrung her cloth in the water. 'Do you think you can walk?'

I nodded. I wasn't sure, but I knew I had to be fit enough for work tomorrow.

She stood up and backed away to the door. 'Come for some food when you are ready.'

I watched her walk away and finished the tea. It had a faint taste of lemongrass and ginger, and already my head was feeling better.

I joined Kham and his family at the meal table. Mr Sone and Kham's brother had changed from their oiled work clothes. The table was laid with steaming rice and meatballs and a bowl of shredded salad.

Mrs Sone pushed a plate towards me. 'How are you now?'

'Fine,' I said. I didn't want them thinking I couldn't work tomorrow.

Moon Bear

Kham was watching me. I wondered if he'd put a bet that I'd drop my food on the table.

Mrs Sone was a good cook. Her fish paste was almost as good as Ma's. I tasted hot chilli, garlic and ginger, all the things Ma cooked at home.

Kham leant across towards me. 'My brother said before you came here, that you would eat like a pig. He said you'd need a trough to eat from.'

'Kham!' Mrs Sone glared at him.

Kham leant even closer and lowered his voice. 'He said you wouldn't know how to use the toilet too.'

'Kham!' Mr Sone rapped his spoon on the table. 'Enough.'

I rolled my rice into a ball and stared into my food. Was that really what they thought of people from the mountains? Did they think we lived like animals?

Mr Sone sat back in his chair and dabbed his mouth. 'So, Tam, what is the Doctor like to work for?'

Kham and Rami stopped mid-mouthful to look at me. They all knew the Doctor. I didn't want them to know I was scared of him. If he found out I didn't like him, I could lose my job. 'The Doctor is a good boss,' I said. 'I am lucky to have him.'

Mr Sone glanced at his wife. 'Well, that is good,' he said. 'I am happy to hear he treats you well.'

We ate in silence. Outside the traffic was still busy. Horns sounded out across the street.

'Is he a real doctor?' I asked.

Mr Sone looked at me. 'He went to college.'

Rami stifled a laugh. 'For one year,' he said. 'His father paid for him to go to medical school, but he got thrown out.'

Mr Sone shifted in his seat. 'We don't know for sure.'

'You can buy your way into college,' said Rami. 'But you can't buy brains.'

Mr Sone glared at him. 'Be careful what you say. His father owns the logging trucks that use our garage. He is a good client. We can't afford to lose his business.'

Rami finished his food and got up to leave. He lifted his motorcycle helmet from behind the door.

His ma cleared the bowls. 'Don't be late back.'

Kham got up to leave too.

'Kham,' said Mr Sone. 'Before you go, I have a job for you.'

Kham groaned, as if he knew just what job his father had in mind.

Mr Sone left the room to his office and came back with a pile of leaflets. He pushed some money across the table. 'That's how much I'll pay you. I won't negotiate the price.'

Moon Bear

Kham stuffed the money in his pocket and picked up the leaflets. I got up to leave too and Kham's ma pushed a bowl of bananas towards me.

'Take one for later,' she said.

I thanked her and took one, glad to get back to the peace of my own room.

I'd hardly sat down on my mattress when Kham knocked and burst through the door. He was carrying the pack of leaflets. He shut the door and sat down next to me.

'Now then, Tam.' He glanced at the door as if he expected someone to follow him. He held up the leaflets. 'How would you like to earn a bit of money for yourself?'

I frowned at him. I could see where this was going, but I could do with the money.

'OK,' said Kham. He leant forward, holding up the money. 'I have a deal. You distribute the leaflets and I'll pay you half of this.'

I looked at him. It hardly seemed fair.

Kham could see I wasn't convinced. 'It happens all the time in business,' he said. 'I'm the middleman.'

I stared at the money in his hands. He was offering me half of it.

'Take it or leave it,' he said.

I needed the money. 'I'll take it,' I said.

Kham grinned. 'Then, my friend, we have ourselves a deal.'

I didn't mind delivering the leaflets. Kham said he'd come with me this first time, to make sure I didn't get knocked down again. It gave me a chance to get out and see some of the city and ease my bruised legs. I followed him along the streets leading towards the city centre. I shoved leaflet after leaflet under car and truck windscreens. The leaflets showed a picture of Kham's father standing next to shiny motor-bikes and cars for sale. He was dressed in a suit and looked much younger than he did in real life.

We passed roadside stalls setting up for the night-time markets. There were stalls selling cooked meats and snacks, and others selling washing powder and brushes and soap. I slowed at one stall to look at embroideries and silks in colours I hadn't seen before. Ma would love it here. I thought that if I ever earned enough money I would come back here and buy these for Ma. I took the money Kham had given me and bought a spool of silver thread. Maybe I could buy one every time I delivered leaflets.

The sun was setting as we headed back. The air was thick with the scent of sandalwood and cedar. At the far end of some streets I caught glimpses of the Mekong, a strip of burnt orange reflecting the sunset sky. I walked back, hands in pockets. I had the spool of silver thread and a little money for myself. For the first time in my life, I felt rich.

In my room I peered across at the bear farm, hidden in darkness, silent too. I wondered about Mama Bear. She hadn't eaten all day. I felt for the keys on the string beneath my shirt.

No one would know.

I stuffed the banana and the flashlight Kham had given me into my pocket and kept in the shadows as I crossed the road to the bear farm. I glanced around to check no one was watching, then unlocked the padlock and slipped through the gates. I pulled open the sliding door of the bear building. It was dark inside, dark and silent. I didn't dare put on the lights. Someone might see from outside. I couldn't hear the bears. What if they had got loose? What if Biter had found his way out of his cage and was waiting for me?

I reached into my pocket for the torch and shone it ahead of me and walked along the aisle between the bears. I could hear their steady breath as I passed.

'It's only me, bears,' I said in a low voice. I squashed the banana beneath my fingers so Mama Bear would find it easier to eat. I shone the flashlight in the cages as I passed. Bear eyes reflected back, like small moons. Biter growled, low growls deep from inside his chest.

I reached Mama Bear's cage. Her fur was pressed against the bars, her paw outstretched towards me. I shone my torch into her eyes, but they were glazed and dull.

Her outstretched paw was cold and stiff.

I felt a sickness deep inside.

I scrunched my hand into her fur and closed my eyes.

I felt it was my fault somehow, that I'd let her down.

Mama Bear was dead.

CHAPTER 13

The Doctor was furious.

He paced up and down between the cages and glared at me. 'You've been here less than a week and already we have a dead bear.'

I stared at the floor. I clenched my hands in fists. I'd told him Mama Bear was sick, but he'd done nothing. I could see Asang out of the corner of my eye. He was keeping his head down, hosing the drainage channel, even though I'd already swept it clean this morning before he'd arrived.

The Doctor kicked a bucket across the concrete, scattering bear food. It clanged against the far wall, spinning the gruel of watery rice across the floor. The bears jumped and hooted in their cages. The Doctor lifted Mama Bear's head and dropped it down again. 'How much do you think it costs to buy another bear?'

I swallowed hard.

'Too much,' spat the Doctor. 'I can't afford a new bear and I will get less money now with one less bear, so you two will get less. Understand?'

Asang kept his eyes on the ground and kept on with his sweeping. I just stared at Mama Bear, kept staring until the Doctor turned on his heels and walked away.

Through the bars, I watched him walk out into the yard and cross to the office. The bears stared after him, panting in their cages and turning tight circles. I hoped the Doctor would get on his motorbike and leave us for the day, but the beep of a car horn stopped him as a sleek black car slid through the open gateway. An armed guard climbed out and opened the passenger door for a suited man to step out onto the yard. The suited man straightened out his jacket and brushed the creases from his trousers. I recognized him, even though he wasn't in his General's uniform. I stepped behind the doors and looked through the crack to get a better view.

I turned to Asang. 'I know that man.'

'General Chan?' He leant on his broom and looked at me. 'Everyone knows the General.'

Moon Bear

I frowned and watched the Doctor and General Chan walk into the office. 'What's he doing here?'

'General Chan comes every week,' said Asang.

I watched the General leave the office carrying a packet and climb back in his car. The window slid up and he was hidden behind the tinted glass.

Asang lit his cigarette. 'General Chan's daughter is sick. He comes every week for bear bile. The doctors say it is the only thing that can save her now.'

I couldn't imagine General Chan having a daughter. I thought of Mae and Sulee. How would I know if they were sick? Would the General know? Would he tell me? Would he even remember who I was?

Asang drew on his cigarette and flicked the ash onto the floor. I watched the smoke spiral upwards and escape through the skylights to the small patch of blue beyond. I wondered if Mama Bear had ever seen the sky, if she'd seen the moon or felt the earth under her feet.

'What will happen to Mama Bear now?' I asked.

Asang glared through the open sliding doors at the Doctor. 'He'll sell her gall bladder to Mr Phomasack at the medicine shop. He'll sell her meat and fur to the market and her paws to the top hotels where they like to serve bear-paw soup.' He stubbed his cigarette on the floor. 'The

Doctor will get his money back and more. There is no need to dock our pay.'

Asang hauled Mama Bear onto the trolley and wheeled her away. I didn't want to see what he did with her. I said I'd feed the other bears. I scraped what I could of the rice from the floor. The bears plunged their noses into their feed trays and slurped with their toothless gums. I sprayed them with water from the hose and let them lick it from their fur. I tried to get Mama Bear's cub to eat, but he wouldn't eat at all. He turned his back. He didn't sway from side to side or bang his head against the bars. He lay still, his head on his huge paws, just staring through the bars at the stained dark concrete of the wall.

Life at the bear farm gave way to routine. I'd be at the farm by dawn, cleaning and feeding the bears. Asang hardly came in. He made sure he came the days the Doctor came. Twice a week, the Doctor would come to milk the bears. I grew to hate those days as much as the bears did. When they saw the Doctor and heard his metal bar clang along their bars, they'd hoot and moan. Biter would slash the air with his claws. He'd lash at anyone: Asang, the Doctor, and even me.

Moon Bear

I learned how to bottle the bear bile and how to dry it out to make bear bile flakes and powders. The Doctor packaged it all to take across the border to his hometown in Vietnam. He said they paid double for bear bile there. General Chan came every week for bile for his daughter. He always saw me, but I don't think he recognized me. I was sure he'd forgotten who I was.

I'd wait for the Doctor to leave and I'd go back to the bear farm late in the evenings to take fruit I'd bought at the market with the money I earned from Kham's father. I'd feed the bears papaya and banana. They liked melon, too. It wouldn't fit through the bars, so I'd have to unbolt the cages, open the door just a crack and slip it in. It took them ages to bite into the round sides. It didn't slip through the bars and it became a game to them, patting the melon with their paws, chasing it around their cage. I think even Mama's cub seemed to like his melon. I never dared open Biter's cage. I cut melon up for him instead.

The bears got to know me. I'd call out, 'It's me, bears, only me.' And they snuffled their noses against the bars, putting paws through for treats of fruit. I got to know the bears too, not just Biter and Mama's cub, but all seven of them, all their different characters.

I gave them names instead of the numbers on their cages. There were Jem and Jep, two brothers, I thought. When they slept, they liked to press against the bars to be as close as possible, paws outstretched towards each other. There was Mii, a huge female bear. She only had three paws and fur was missing from her head and all around her back. I often saw her sitting on her haunches pulling out great tufts of hair. Nok had a missing paw too. She liked to watch the small birds that sometimes fluttered high up in the roof space. She would lie on her back and stare upwards all day long. Hua was a young bear, the smallest in the farm. He was the clown. He liked to roll over and over when I was near. He'd hoot and mock charge at me when I walked near his cage and if I ever dared to come too close he'd swat me with his paw.

Some evenings, I'd run other errands for Kham. I'd sweep his father's garage yard and clean and polish the cars. The yard was always busy, a steady stream of cars and lorries and especially the logging trucks, brought in for new tyres or brakes or bust axles. I spent some of the money I earned on the fruit and treats for the bears, but I also saved enough to buy a bolt of red cloth that I knew Ma would like. If I saved hard enough, maybe I could even pay for a trip to take it to her.

Moon Bear

Then one evening, when I was helping Kham to clean his father's car, three logging trucks rolled in. Kham rubbed his hands and grinned. We'd earn good money cleaning these. I watched the trucks' huge wheels roll past us, covered in the red mud of the forests, bringing the deep rich smell of the earth. A place that felt so far and distant from me now.

I closed my eyes and breathed in deeply, filling my lungs.

I wanted to be back in the forests. I wanted to find a way back to the mountains and the deep rich earth, but it seemed an impossible dream.

I didn't know it, but bundled in a crate and hidden in a space beneath the last truck that rolled in, Good Luck had just arrived.

Chapter 14

I was surprised to see the Doctor at the garage yard that evening. He pulled up on his motorbike by Mr Sone's house. The sun had set behind the roofline and only a thin strip of gold lay in the western sky. The yard floodlights threw long double shadows across the yard. The Doctor walked across, swinging his hips, his thumbs hooked in his back pockets.

Mr Sone put his head up from the bonnet of a car and I could see Mrs Sone watching from her window. I glanced at Kham and put my cloth back into the bucket and stepped away from his father's car. I didn't want the Doctor to think I was earning money from Mr Sone too.

A man from one of the logging trucks jumped down from his cab to meet the Doctor. I recognized him from the logging station when I'd gone with Pa to trade bush meat with the workers. He was a big man with a tiger tattoo on his shoulder and greased-back hair. I stepped into the shadows and watched them deep in talk. I could see the Doctor shaking his head and turn to walk away. He walked slowly, kicking up the dust with his heels. The lorry driver called him back and spoke some more and pointed to his truck.

The Doctor turned in my direction. 'Mountain Boy,' he yelled. 'Over here.'

I glanced at Kham. I didn't think the Doctor had seen me here. I wiped my hands on my shorts and walked across the yard. The Doctor paced in circles. 'Help them get the crate,' he barked.

I followed the lorry driver and crouched with him beneath the truck. Between the huge wheels, a small wooden crate was fixed to the underside of the truck with metal brackets. The cab driver pulled out the crate and I helped him slide it across the ground to rest in front of the Doctor.

The Doctor put his hands on his hips and kicked the crate. 'Open it.'

The lorry driver slid the top of the crate to the side and we all peered in. Even Kham had plucked up courage to come and look. At first all I could see was a bundle of old towels and a few chunks of squashed banana. The towels squirmed and moved. Something was beneath them. The towels were stained with a yellowish stinking liquid. I covered my nose to hide the smell.

A small black paw poked out from beneath the towels. A dog? A puppy? The lorry driver pulled the towels away and dumped them on the ground beside him. But I couldn't take my eyes from the creature inside the crate. It was almost puppy-like, but too big to be one of the village pups of home. It was curled up, with fine black hair covering the folds of skin across its body, folds of skin it would have to grow into. Its nose and mouth were soft and pink. Its short chunky legs ended in large paws with fine needle-like claws. The pads were soft and hairless, creased and pink. It wasn't a puppy at all.

The Doctor reached in and pulled on one paw to turn the creature over, showing the crescent of white fur on its chest.

I sank down on my knees and held onto the side of the crate.

It was a moon bear cub, the bear cub I'd seen on the mountain. It had grown since I'd seen it, but it had the whorl of white hairs that looked just like the evening star. This was the bear cub from home.

Moon Bear

It lay in its own filth. Pasty yellow diarrhoea stuck to the fur around its bottom.

This cub hadn't got away. I wondered what had happened to the mother.

The Doctor kicked the crate again. 'I don't want it,' he said. 'It's sick. It's too young.'

The cub mewled softly and tried to push itself against the bare wooden slats of the crate. It seemed too weak to stand.

'It'll be a strong bear one day,' said the lorry driver. 'Look, it's a male bear.'

'It'll be dead by the morning,' said the Doctor.

The driver pointed at the banana. 'It's just hungry. See, it's not eaten. Maybe he'll take some rice.'

The Doctor stared in at the cub. 'How long has it been away from its mother?' said the Doctor.

'One day, maybe two,' said the driver. 'The trappers found it wandering alone on the road.'

The Doctor snorted at his lies.

'This one will bring you good luck and great fortune,' said the driver.

The Doctor curled his lip. 'Good luck?'

The driver nodded. 'Sôok-dìi, they called it. The trappers called it Sôok-dìi. They said it would bring great luck to whoever owned this bear.'

'It would have been better luck if you'd brought me the mother. I'd have paid double for her. Who did you sell her to?'

The driver picked up the towels and threw them back in the crate. 'If you're not interested…'

The Doctor rubbed his chin.

'…then we have someone else who wants this bear.'

The Doctor reached into his back pocket and pulled out a fistful of notes. 'Half price,' he said, holding up the money. 'My father wouldn't want to hear you were selling me sick bears, would he?'

The driver glared at the Doctor. In the box, the bear cub pawed at the damp towels. A trickle of yellow diarrhoea tinged with blood dribbled out around its small stump of a tail.

'OK,' said the driver. He snatched the money from the Doctor. 'Half price, for you only.'

The Doctor gave me a shove. 'Pick up the bear.'

I looked at him.

'Pick it up.'

I crouched down to the bear. How do you pick up a bear? It had grown since I'd seen it in the bear den. Did it have teeth at this age? Its back end was matted and stank like the latrines back home when sickness had swept through the village. I reached in behind its neck and grabbed the folds of loose skin. The cub twisted and squirmed. He squealed and opened his jaws, but I could see his teeth were tiny needle-sharp bumps poking through his gums and I could see the suckling groove in its upper lip. This cub was still feeding from his mother.

I lifted him up by the scruff of his neck and wrapped him in one of the dirty towels. The driver took the crate and slung it on the lorry and turned his back on us.

The Doctor looked at the cub in my arms. He put his hand across his nose to hide the smell. 'Take him back to the farm and give him food and water. He can have Mama Bear's cage.'

'Yes, Doctor,' I said.

I turned round. Kham and his family had come to look at the bear cub too.

I walked with the Doctor across the yard.

When he reached his motorbike he stopped. 'And Mountain Boy ...'

I turned.

The Doctor swung his leg across the bike and pulled on his leather gloves. 'Don't let it die. If it dies tonight, you can pack your bags and go.'

I watched the Doctor rev his engine and spin out of the yard. Kham and his brother stood behind me.

Mrs Sone glared at her husband. 'I thought we said no more bears in this yard.'

Mr Sone shrugged his shoulders. 'What can I do? Anyway, look. It is only a small one.'

Mrs Sone flapped her arms at me. 'Take it. Take it away. I don't want bears here, understand?'

The cub was struggling in the towel. I walked past them and crossed the road, glad it wasn't busy. I unlocked the gates, pulled open the sliding doors and switched on the lights.

'Sôok-dìi!' I said. I held the cub at arm's length by the scruff of its neck. 'Sôok-dìi! I hope you live up to your name.'

The cub's paws paddled the air.

I couldn't lose my job. I had to send money back to Ma. I couldn't let this bear cub die.

I needed all the luck I could get.

CHAPTER 15

What was I going to do with a bear cub?

I carried him to Mama Bear's old cage. The other bears shuffled in their cages, expecting their usual evening treats of fruit.

'No fruit today,' I called out.

Hua tried to swat me as I passed. Biter stuck his nose through the bars and held his nose up high, sniffing the new scent of bear.

'He stinks,' I said. 'We'd better give him a bath, hadn't we?'

All the bears were sitting on their haunches, watching me, or rather watching the new bear. Mama Bear's son lifted his head from his paws to peer at the newcomer too.

I lifted Sôok-dìi into Mama Bear's cage and closed the door. The cub was too small for the bars. His stumpy legs slipped and slid. He was too weak to balance and he wedged himself between the lower bars.

I uncoiled the long hose and began to wash him with water. He wriggled and mewled. I let the water run until his back end was clean and water dripped from the dark fur.

'Tam! It's me, Kham!'

Kham was calling me from outside the sliding doors.

I left the water running and went to find him. He was standing at the entrance to the bear barn, wide-eyed and ready to run.

He didn't take his eyes from the row of bears. 'Are they all locked in?'

I nodded.

'My father sent me to say he is locking the yard gates soon. So don't be late back.'

I looked back at Sôok-dìi at the end of the row. I'd have to hurry. 'I'll come soon,' I said.

Kham took one look at me and left.

I rolled up the hose and went back to Sôok-dìi. His eyes were closed and he was shivering. He was sucking on his front paws just like Sulee used to suck her thumb. His legs hung through the bars. He couldn't move. I looked across at Biter. It was hard to imagine Sôok-dìi could grow that big.

Right,' I said. 'You need food.'

I fetched some bananas from the prep room and mashed them in my fingers. I tried to feed little pieces through the bars, but Sôok-dìi turned his nose away and the pieces dropped onto the floor. I could see him drifting into sleep. I opened the cage door and tried to wake him. I could feel his ribs beneath his soft fur. I guessed he hadn't fed in a while. I tried him with another piece of banana, but instead he tried to hold my fingers in his paws and tried to suckle them.

I looked back towards where Kham had been standing. I couldn't just leave this bear cub. He could be dead by the morning. Maybe if I took him back for one night I could try and feed him through the night. I knew Mrs Sone wouldn't allow me, but she needn't know. I wondered what Ma would have thought too. We never let animals inside our house.

I grabbed an old towel from the prep room and wrapped Sôok-dìi inside. He wriggled and squirmed at first but then lay still. I took a banana and a papaya and locked up the farm and left.

Mr Sone waved to me as I walked into the yard. I kept my head down and wrapped my arm tightly around the bundle in my arms. I hoped he wouldn't call me over and was glad the bundle didn't wriggle and give itself away.

I shut the door of my room behind me, leaning my back against it. I could hear Mr Sone's footsteps in the yard outside. I held my breath. I heard him shut the garage gates and bolt and chain them. His footsteps turned in the direction of his house. I breathed out. I was safe. No one would disturb me now. The logging lorries had gone, their broken tyres replaced for another trip into the forests.

I switched on the light, sank to the floor and unwrapped the bear cub from the towel. He blinked, his small eyes barely open. I broke another piece of banana and covered my fingers in banana paste, but Sôok-dìi didn't seem to want it. He stretched his small paws and squirmed onto my lap as if he was trying to push himself right into me. His paws kneaded against my T-shirt and he nuzzled against my chest.

I lifted my hand and ran it across the soft fur on the top of his head. Beneath his folds of loose skin, I could feel the ridged bumps of his backbone and ribs beneath his fur. His stomach felt hollow and empty and I wondered just how long ago he'd eaten.

Moon Bear

Close up his muzzle smelt sour, like the smell on the buffalo calves when they'd gorged themselves on their mothers' milk. Maybe he wasn't on solid food yet at all. He must have been feeding from his mother when he was taken. I didn't have any milk. I wondered if baby milk would do. I remember one of Ma's cousins needing powdered milk to feed her baby. She had to travel far to find it. Maybe I could feed Sôok-dìi like that too, although I didn't know where to get milk or even how much it would cost. I tried to think what bears would eat in the forest. Fruit and roots and grubs. But then I remembered what Grandfather told me about bears. They go mad for honey. I left Sôok-dìi curled up in the towel and opened the small cupboard. I reached in for the tin of honey I swore I wouldn't open. Forest honey. Bear honey. I didn't suppose a little would matter, to give some to the bear cub.

I turned the lid and scooped up a fingerful of honey. I could see the honeycomb inside still filled with bee grubs. I crouched down and slid my finger inside Sôok-dìi's mouth. At first he shook his head and tried to spit it out, but once he'd tasted the sweet honey, he pushed himself closer.

I smiled. 'You want some more?'

He sniffed it and licked a little from my fingers. I wondered if he remembered the taste of honey. Maybe his mother had brought a comb of honey and shared it with him. I wondered, if like me, the taste of it took him back to the forest. He wriggled closer for another taste. I scraped out nearly half the pot for him and he sucked and sucked the sweet honey from my hand. I dipped my fingers in the water of my washbowl and let him lick the water off my fingers too.

He tried to crawl up my chest and sleep in the crook of my neck.

'No you don't,' I said.

I folded the towel in the corner of the room and wrapped him up inside it.

'You can sleep there tonight.'

I switched out the light and curled up under my own sheet. I closed my eyes and hoped sleep would find me. I was falling asleep as I felt him crawl against me, snuffling and pawing his way into me. He gave a low humming sound from deep inside his chest, and curled up, resting the flat of his paw against my cheek. I could feel his fast heartbeat through his rib-thin chest. I wondered how he'd been taken. A cub this young couldn't wander from its mother. I stared up through the small skylight, to a thin sliver of moon. It was a crescent moon, like the white crescent on his chest. It was the same moon that hung over the forest canopies and reflected in the still waters below the waterfalls where I'd seen him in his den. I thought of Grandfather. Maybe he was looking up through the branches of the trees at the same moon right now and thinking of me too.

I pushed my face into Sôok-dìi's soft fur and breathed in the deep scent of the earth, of the leaf litter, of the forest paths and the cool mountain rain. I closed my eyes and let the images fill the room and shine brightly in the darkness.

I belonged there. Sôok-dìi belonged there too.

I curled my arm around him. 'One day,' I said. 'I promise you. I'll make sure we both get back home again.'

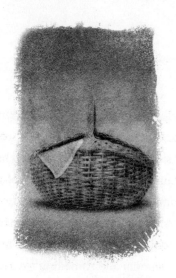

Chapter 16

I woke spluttering and coughing, unable to breathe. Sôok-dìi had squirmed onto my face and had his muzzle pressed against my nose. I pushed him off and sat up. It was still dark outside but the heady scent of sandalwood from the monasteries drifted on the early morning air. This was usually my favourite time, when the air was clear of dust and I could watch the stars fade in the dawn sky. But today I had no time to lie and listen to the city wake.

I had a bear to feed.

I switched on the light and Sôok-dìi squinted at the brightness. He seemed a little stronger than yesterday. He could stand, but when he tried to scamper across the room he fell over. He took the honey tin between his paws and stretched his long pink tongue inside to lick out what he could

Moon Bear

find. Somehow, I'd have to find more food for him today. I'd have to wash the dirty towels too. Mrs Sone would probably throw me out if she knew a bear was sleeping in here.

I could hear Mr Sone unlock the garage gates and waited until I guessed he had returned to the house. I pushed open the door to my room. I could see Kham and his family through the window of their house in the white neon light. Kham's brother was already near the door. He'd be out in the yard soon. I couldn't risk anybody stopping to talk to me. I wrapped Sôok-dìi in a towel and reached for the money I earned from errands for Kham. There wasn't much left after buying that bolt of red cloth for Ma. It couldn't be helped. I'd have to try and buy some milk today. I tucked Sôok-dìi beneath my arm and raced across the road before the sun had even risen above the rooftops.

It was Saturday. Neither Asang nor the Doctor came on Saturdays, but I wondered if the Doctor might drop in to check on the new cub. I didn't even know where the Doctor lived or where he went at the weekends. Mr and Mrs Sone said he went back across to Vietnam to see his family, but Kham's brother said he had a girlfriend across the Friendship Bridge in Thailand.

Asang hardly ever came in to see the bears. He left that to me. He'd bring sacks of rice and fruits, but sometimes he forgot and I'd have to try and ration out the rice until he brought some more.

The bears turned as I walked in. They lifted their noses, smelling the new bear curled up against me. Maybe it brought some memories of forests for them too. Sôok-dìi squirmed and mewled in my arms. I'd have to find milk for him. Cleaning would have to wait. He was too small for Mama Bear's cage, so I decided to take him with me while I went to buy the milk. I couldn't chance him slipping through the bars. I put him in a rattan basket, covered him with a couple of towels and headed out onto the street.

'Hey, Tam!'

I turned. Kham was following me up the road.

'Where are you going?'

I kept walking, wrapping my arms around the basket. Sôok-dìi was hidden in the folds of towel. I didn't want Kham to see.

'I have to get food for the bears,' I said. It was true enough. I'd meant to buy them some fruit.

'I'll come,' he said.

I kept on walking. 'I'm just fine by myself.'

Moon Bear

Kham jogged to catch up and walked along beside me, kicking the dirt. 'We need to find a way of making money.'

'I thought you were selling stuff at school.'

Kham tutted. 'They banned me. A teacher said it wasn't school policy, but I think it's just because he got a flashlight that didn't work.'

'Oh!' I said.

I kept our pace striding slightly ahead of him.

'Is that all you can say, "oh"?'

I stopped at a junction and looked both ways for traffic. 'What do you want me to say?'

Kham trotted across the road with me. 'Well how did your family earn money?'

I could feel Sôok-dìi wriggling inside the basket and heard him sucking on his paws. I just hoped he'd go back to sleep. I frowned and thought back. Money wasn't something we thought about, that much. 'We didn't need much,' I said, 'though Ma sold her embroidery, and Pa…' I stopped talking. I hadn't spoken of Pa since I'd left the village. I quickened my pace. It was hard here walking in the city. Fast steps and slow steps, dodging the people and the traffic, not like the long easy strides through the forest.

Kham trotted to keep up with me. 'What about your Pa?'

I just wished Kham would go away. I could feel Sôok-dìi bump about in the basket. I glanced down to see him wriggle free of the towels and claw his way to the basket edge. His head was poking out. I slipped into a side street and slid down behind some bins.

Kham ducked in behind me. 'Tam! What are you...?'

His eyes opened wider as he stared at the bear cub I was trying to push back into the basket.

He took a back step. 'Tam!' he said slowly, stringing out my name. 'Is that...the bear?'

I frowned and tried to cover the cub, but he pawed his way out.

'What are you doing with it?'

I looked around. 'Don't tell everyone,' I snapped.

I swaddled the bear like I'd seen Ma do with my baby sisters, wrapping one of the towels tight around him, tucking his paws against the folds. He couldn't move. I laid him back in the basket and brought the other towel over him to hide him from view.

Kham was still staring at me.

'I have to find it some milk,' I said. 'Baby milk.' I stuck my head out of the side alley and looked up and down the street. 'But I don't know where to find any.'

Moon Bear

I looked back at Kham, but he just stood, grinning at me.

'What?' I said.

Kham laughed and slapped me on the back. 'You know Tam,' he said, 'life's been a whole lot more fun since you arrived. Come on, I know where to get your milk.'

I followed him along two more streets until we stood outside the window of a pharmacy.

'In here?' I said.

Kham peered in through the glass doors and nodded. 'I know the shopkeeper. Let me do the talking.'

I stood inside the pharmacy, looking around. Inside, the walls were filled with boxes, bottles and pill pots and lotions. There were even some pots with the bear farm logo. I wondered if the Doctor sold bear bile here too.

'Kham!' The lady at the counter greeted Kham with a huge smile.

Kham smiled back.

'And how are your parents, Kham?'

'They are very well, thank you,' he said. He glanced back at me and frowned. I could feel Sôok-dìi wriggling against the basket. I could hear his claws scraping in the rattan. I hoped he wasn't getting out of the towel.

'My friend,' said Kham, pointing at me, 'would like some powdered milk for his baby sister.'

My eyebrows shot up my forehead.

Sôok-dìi gave a mewling cry and the shopkeeper latched her eyes on the basket.

'His mother is too sick to come,' Kham added.

Other customers turned to listen too. One lady smiled and tried to peer inside the basket.

The shopkeeper's face softened. She reached up behind her and pulled two boxes. 'Newborn or for six months plus?'

I stared at Kham.

'Newborn,' said Kham nodding at me.

I nodded too. 'Newborn.'

She held up a feeding bottle. 'And one of these?'

'No,' said Kham.

'Yes,' I said.

The shopkeeper looked between us and showed us the total on her till. I dug deep into my pockets and pulled out all the money I had. Kham counted it out.

He glanced at me. 'It's not enough.'

I looked at him. 'It's all I have.'

Kham fished into his own pockets. 'I don't have any either.'

Moon Bear

Sôok-dìi cried out again, a strange strangled cry. I could see him wriggling from the towel; a small black paw was free. The people in the queue behind us were looking at the basket.

I pulled the towel to cover Sôok-dìi. 'It's OK,' I said. I started backing towards the door.

Kham glanced down at the basket. He pulled a sad face. 'His sister has the sickness too.'

The shopkeeper put her head on one side and looked at me and then at the basket. 'Here,' she said, lifting the box of milk and the bottle and stepping around the counter, 'take this to your mother.'

She smiled and tried to peer in the basket.

'It's catching,' said Kham pushing me out of the door. 'We'd better go.'

'Thank you,' I called out, but Kham was already marching me down the road back to the bear farm.

'That was close,' he grinned.

'You lied,' I said. 'To get the milk, you lied.'

'It was a small lie.' Kham shrugged his shoulders. 'Everyone lies, Tam. Anyway, you have your milk.'

We walked fast. The basket was heavy in my arms and I could tell Sôok-dìi's cries were ones of hunger.

'Where do you keep the cub?' asked Kham. 'Where does he sleep at night?'

'In a cage,' I said. 'He sleeps in a cage next to the other bears.'

Everyone lies, I thought.

Even me.

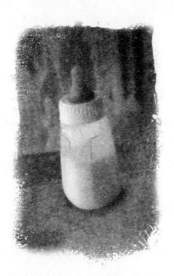

Chapter 17

Kham came back with me to the bear farm to help me read the instructions for making up the milk from powder. Sôok-dìi sat between us on the floor.

Kham looked beyond me into the bear barn. 'They can't escape, can they?'

'There's a bolt across each cage,' I said.

Kham looked unconvinced. 'My brother said that the last worker got mauled because a bear opened up its own cage and got out. Did you know that?'

I looked at him to see if he was trying to scare me.

He didn't look as if he was joking. 'They can work things in their paws, bears. Can't they?' he said.

Biter's cage had a metal peg through the bolt. Maybe it was Biter who had mauled a man.

Sôok-dìi snuffled at my ankles and tried to chew my gumboots.

'Come on,' I said. 'We need to feed Sôok-dìi.'

Kham held up the box of powdered milk and read out the instructions. I measured out the milk powder and stirred it into warm water in the bottle.

'How old d'you think he is?' asked Kham.

I shrugged my shoulders. I tried to work out just how long it was since I'd seen him in the bear den. 'He must be about three months old,' I said.

Kham frowned. 'It says here that you'll have to feed him every three hours.'

'Every three!' I said. 'How much do I have to give each time?'

Kham turned the packet over in his hands, reading the words. 'Dunno,' he laughed. 'Doesn't say anything about bears here.'

I scowled at him and screwed the bottle top with the milking teat on top. I shook the milk bottle and watched the powder dissolve into the warm water.

'How you going to get him to drink that?' said Kham.

I picked up Sôok-dìi and held him in the crook of my arm like I'd seen Ma cradle my baby sisters. I pushed the bottle teat into his mouth. At first he pulled away, but the taste of milk was on his tongue and he nosed forward trying to lick the teat. Soon he put his paws either side of the bottle as if holding it for himself and drank and drank until the bottle was empty. He still sucked the teat as if he wanted more.

'He's still hungry,' said Kham.

'I'll give him some more later.' I remembered the way Mae used to be sick after feeds. I didn't want him being sick too.

I carried Sôok-dìi back to Mama Bear's old cage. He was sleepy after the milk and the morning's walk into the town. At least I'd be able to clean and feed the bears while he slept. I found an old plastic crate, lined it with the towel and placed it inside the cage. It would be more comfortable in the crate than on the bare bars.

I returned to the prep room to wash the bottle and find somewhere to hide the milk powder. I didn't want the Doctor to see, in case he tried to stop me.

Kham was in the prep room pressing at the buttons of the ultrasound machine.

'Don't touch,' I yelled.

Kham spun round and lifted his hands from the machine. 'What does it do?'

'It shows pictures inside the body. It shows the Doctor where the gall bladder is,' I said, 'so he can push a needle right inside and drain the bile.'

'Can you work it?'

'Yes.' I'd learned which buttons to press when the Doctor scanned the bellies of the bears.

'Well, come on then,' said Kham getting up. 'Let's have a go.'

I frowned. 'You can't just get the bears out and scan them,' I said.

Kham laughed and lifted up his shirt. 'Not the bears. Try me.'

'You?'

Kham lifted up his shirt. 'Scan me.'

I looked beyond the door to the empty yard. 'OK,' I laughed.

I switched on the machine and watched the small screen flicker into life. I lifted the probe and rubbed some gel on its end and pointed it at Kham.

Kham backed away. 'This isn't going to hurt, is it?'

'Not this bit,' I said.

Kham lifted his shirt again and I ran the probe across his belly. I'd watched the Doctor do this before. The probe slipped across Kham's skin. The hazy white screen of his liver gave way to a round black hole.

I stared at the screen. 'That's your gall bladder,' I said.

'Where?' he said.

I shoved my finger hard in his belly, 'There!'

'Ow!' cried Kham. He pushed me away. 'That hurt.'

'MOUNTAIN BOY!'

I spun round. I hadn't heard a motorbike arrive in the yard. I hadn't heard footsteps on the concrete outside the door. My heart pounded in my chest.

The Doctor stood in the doorway, the long metal bar swinging from his hand.

CHAPTER 18

'So this is what I pay you for. To play games?'

I glanced at Kham, but his eyes were firmly on the floor.

The Doctor took another step towards me. 'The bears are not fed. The floors are not cleaned. What do you think you are doing?'

'The cub is well,' I said. 'I've been feeding the cub.'

The Doctor whipped the back of his hand across my face. 'The cub isn't earning his keep at the moment.' He spat on the floor. 'And neither are you.'

My cheek burned and my eyes stung with angry tears. I was angry at Kham too. I shouldn't have mucked around with him. He had nothing to lose, but I had everything. My family needed me. Ma needed the money I earned.

Moon Bear

'I'm sorry,' I said. I wiped the end of the probe and started to pack the ultrasound away.

'Leave it out,' he snapped. 'General Chan is coming shortly. Make sure you stay. I will need you, as Asang is not here today.'

He turned and left the room, leaving Kham and me in deep silence. My heart was still thumping in my chest and my legs felt weak and shaky.

Kham stared wide-eyed after the Doctor. 'I'm so sorry,' he said.

I turned my back on him and turned on the taps to wash the milk bottle. 'Just go,' I said.

'Tam, really …'

'Just go,' I snapped. I swirled water into the bottle, the pressure from the tap making the water spray out from the top. 'You'll get me in more trouble if you stay.'

I shook the bottle hard, listening to his footsteps fade away.

How could I have been so stupid? Of all the times the Doctor could have come back, why now? I rinsed the bottle, hid it at the back of a cupboard and went to feed the bears.

The bears were restless. Mama Bear's cub swayed faster to and fro. Jem and Jep copied, swinging side to side at the back of their cages, grunting and hooting. I turned the hose and flushed the water beneath the cages washing out the night's remains. I was glad I hadn't given them fruit the night before. I didn't want the Doctor to find I'd been giving them extra treats. I brushed down the concrete, flushing all the waste into the drains, careful to keep out of the Doctor's way.

The Doctor seemed restless too. I could see him pacing in the yard, checking his watch. He stood back and slicked his hair as General Chan's car slid into the compound. The driver climbed out of the front and opened the passenger door. General Chan brushed his trousers and stepped across the yard, careful where he put his feet.

The Doctor went to greet him, and then instead of taking him to the office, they walked towards me, towards the bear barn. General Chan's gaze passed over me. He frowned as if he knew me from somewhere but couldn't place me. I wanted to ask him how my mother and sisters were. But I knew we were probably nothing to him.

General Chan walked with the Doctor along the row of cages, stopping to inspect each bear. He stared in at Mama Bear's cub. 'The pills and powders you sell me are not working.'

The Doctor clasped and unclasped his hands. A bead

of sweat trickled down his forehead. 'My bear bile is of the very best quality,' he said.

General Chan prodded Mama Bear's son. The bear moaned and turned away. 'My daughter's doctor says she must have the freshest bile from the strongest bear.'

'They are all strong bears,' insisted the Doctor, 'but let me show you my strongest bear.'

General Chan followed the Doctor along the row of cages. The leather soles of the General's shoes tapped on the concrete in the silence.

When they reached Biter's cage, Biter lashed out and clawed at the air. The General didn't flinch. He stared at Biter and Biter stared back. Saliva frothed from Biter's mouth as he pressed his muzzle against the bars.

'This one,' General Chan said. 'This one is a fighter. He's the one.'

The Doctor smiled, 'A good choice.' He clapped his hands at me. 'Boy, get the trolley. We will milk this one.'

I fetched the trolley from the prep room and pushed it to Biter's cage. The Doctor drew up the sedative and paced around Biter's cage. Biter moaned and hooted and spun round to face the Doctor, clamping his teeth against the bars, his whole body shaking in fury. He lashed out at the injection on the long pole.

But the Doctor was fast and practised. He lunged the injection at Biter's hind legs and Biter snarled as the needle hit home.

'There,' smiled the Doctor. 'You see, he is our strongest bear.'

General Chan nodded, and watched as Biter's head dropped, his legs became shaky and he finally slumped in the cage.

The Doctor prodded him with the stick. 'You cannot be too careful,' he said. But Biter didn't move. His breath came out in a soft snore through the folds of his muzzle. I could tell he was deeply sedated. He'd gone deeper this time, and I wondered if the Doctor had given a bigger dose.

The Doctor opened the cage door and I helped to drag Biter out and slide him onto the trolley. Usually Asang would do this and I realized just how strong he must be. The Doctor and I pulled Biter out by his head and paws and wheeled him to the prep room.

General Chan pulled out a chair and brushed the creases from his trousers. He took his gold-rimmed glasses from a case in the pocket of his shirt, put them on and perched his hands upon his knees. He intended to watch the Doctor milk this bear.

Moon Bear

The Doctor dabbed the sweat from his face and tried to brush the black bear hairs from his white T-shirt. 'A strong bear,' he said, patting Biter's belly.

General Chan stared, unmoved.

I watched the Doctor run the probe across Biter's belly and saw the black circle of the gall bladder come onto the screen. He tried to puncture Biter's belly several times before he found it. I noticed his hands were shaking and he kept glancing at General Chan.

'Ah!' he said at last, and I watched as he fitted the needle to the pump, and watched the black sludge of bile track slowly along the tube into the flask.

I hated watching this.

Instead I fixed my eyes on Biter, on his massive bulk filling up the trolley. His huge pads were like thickened leather. Reddened sores covered his elbows, and his fur was matted and stuck to the skin by a thin film of yellow pus. His open mouth revealed his broken teeth.

I wondered if General Chan saw this. Did he see Biter as strong bear, or the broken warrior that he was?

I helped the Doctor haul Biter back into his cage and slide the bolt, locking him in. Biter's great body was slumped against the bars. He was done for today.

The Doctor lifted the flask of fresh bile up to the

light. 'The freshest bile. This will make your daughter better.' He ran his hands through his hair and smiled, but I noticed he couldn't stop his leg from jiggling on the spot.

General Chan seemed satisfied. He pulled a wallet from his pocket and put a roll of notes on the table. 'I will be looking for my money back if this does not work,' he said.

The Doctor smiled and bowed. 'It is the best bile in all Laos,' he said. 'I have many customers who return again and again.'

General Chan snorted. 'Maybe if it was that good they would have no need to return.'

The Doctor smiled and bowed again, but did not say anything. I noticed the muscles in his mouth clench tight against his jaw. Maybe he didn't trust himself to speak.

General Chan took the flask and swilled the green sludge around inside. 'I hope for your sake that this will work. I wouldn't want to be the one to tell your father you are no better at bear farming than you are at being a doctor.'

I watched General Chan walk out into the bright sunshine of the yard. He had no claws or teeth. I doubted he could run or fight or survive within the jungle, yet here, even the Doctor feared him. In his suit and tie, General Chan was the pinstriped tiger of the city.

I hoped the Doctor would leave too. But he seemed in no mood to go. He picked up the metal bar and walked into the barn swinging it and whacking it against the ground. I could see him stop by Biter's cage. Biter was still under deep sedation. I turned away as the Doctor brought the bar down on Biter. I walked away so that I couldn't see or hear.

The Doctor finally emerged from the bear barn. His face was red. Sweat poured down his face. Veins bulged at his temples.

He slammed the metal bar on the ground and turned to me. 'Clean up the mess in there.'

He swung his leg over his motorbike, roared out onto the road, and was gone.

I stepped into the bear barn. My heart thumped inside my chest. I hoped the Doctor hadn't taken his anger out on Sôok-dìi. I found Biter groaning in his cage. One eye was open. The other was closed and puffed where his face had taken the Doctor's blows. He struggled to lift his head. Drips of blood collected and congealed beneath his cage. I fetched the hose and let the cool water run across his swollen eye and muzzle. I nudged the hose into his mouth hoping the water would soothe the bruises. Biter poked out his tongue to lick the water droplets from his nose.

Biter had fighting spirit in him.

But for how long?

How much more could this big bear take?

Kham and his family were eating their evening meal when I walked into the kitchen. Kham's mother watched me wash my hands and take a seat. She passed a bowl of rice and meat salad. I could feel her eyes burning into me. Did she see me carry the crate across the road? Did she know I'd brought the bear cub and it was in my room right now with the milk bottle and powdered milk?

Kham had stopped eating. He stared down at his food.

His mother leaned across to me. 'Tam, how is the Doctor today?'

'Fine,' I said.

She glanced at Kham. 'Kham says that you almost lost your job today.'

My mouth went dry. Was she about to ask me to leave too?

132

Moon Bear

I noticed Kham's eyes flit in my direction.

'The Doctor was very kind,' I said. 'He let me keep my job.'

Kham's mother looked at her husband. 'Tam, if you find yourself without a job, then you can work here, at the garage. Mr Sone will find you enough work to pay for your keep.'

I looked up at her. 'Thank you,' I said.

She sat back and folded her hands across her knees. She looked at Kham's brother. 'Rami tells us General Chan visited the bear farm today.'

Her tone was casual, but I could hear the questions in it.

'I'd recognize his car anywhere,' said Rami. 'It's the only one of that type in the city. A German import.'

'Difficult to get spares,' said Mr Sone. 'Especially the way he drives it.'

'So?' said Kham's mother.

'So ... if it breaks down ...' said Mr Sone.

Kham's mother tutted. 'No, not that. Why did General Chan make his visit?'

She looked at me but I guessed she knew the answer already.

'He wanted bear bile,' I said.

Mrs Sone wiped her hands on her apron. 'Then it is true what they are saying at the hospital,' she said. 'She is back in Laos.'

'Who?' said Kham.

'General Chan's daughter,' said Mrs Sone. 'His only child. He gives her everything. Treats her like a son.'

Rami leant across and nudged me. 'She doesn't look like a boy. She is the most beautiful girl in all Laos. Maybe in the world. She's been the festival beauty queen twice already.' He leant back and smiled. 'She's intelligent too, doing a degree in engineering in Russia.'

'Well,' said Mrs Sone. 'I hear she is very sick. She had treatment there but it wasn't working. General Chan wants to use traditional Chinese medicine instead.' She looked at me. 'He wants bear bile.'

'Well, I hope it makes her better soon,' I said.

I meant it too. I hoped Biter's bile made General Chan's daughter well again. I wondered just how much she would need. I hoped she'd get better, not for General Chan's sake but for Biter's and mine. What if it didn't work? I'd seen the Doctor take out his anger on the bears.

There was no knowing what he could do.

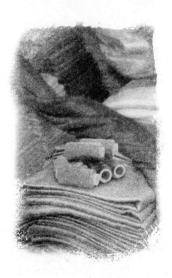

CHAPTER 19

It took me another two months after the incident with Kham and the ultrasound to dare to ask the Doctor for time off. I'd bought threads and rolls of cloth for Ma with the money I earned from Mr Sone, and I had saved some money too. I wanted to go back home to see Ma.

I watched the Doctor through the window of his office. He'd been in a better mood lately. He was running a good trade. When people heard that General Chan's daughter was getting better, they wanted bile from the Doctor's bear farm too. People came for treatments for stomach upsets, sores, chills, and bruises. They came for almost anything. For some it was a tonic, a good luck drink to be washed down with rice whisky at weddings. The Doctor even turned the small office into a shop. Sometimes tourists arrived in minibuses with cameras to have their photo taken with the bears. The Doctor would let them feed the bears fruit on the ends of sticks. He loved to taunt Biter to lash out and show his strength. Biter impressed people. His bile was the priciest of all and the Doctor would label some bottles with Biter's name though I suspected they didn't all contain his bile.

People liked to take photos of Sôok-dìi too. In those two months he'd grown from a wriggling cub, with a fat belly and stubby legs, to a leaner bear cub, a miniature version of the bear he would become. I couldn't keep him in my room any more. He'd tried to chew the bed and mattress and tear up the bolts of cloth for Ma. I hated leaving him in the cage in the bear barn. He'd moan and try to reach me through the bars, or sit with his back turned, sulking and sucking his paws.

I let him out in the barn when I was cleaning and feeding the other bears. He liked to follow me around and put his paws on the cages and sniff at the other bears, although I noticed he never went near Biter. I managed to train him too, with sugared nuts I bought at the market. I could make him sit and lie down and stay. I could make him reach up high, standing on his hind legs. I could make him snarl and bare his teeth and pat the air in front of him. All this, just for sugared nuts.

Moon Bear

I was relieved to be able to feed him the same food as the other bears. The milk was becoming too expensive. I kept one bottle of milk for night time though. Then, he'd curl against me and try to crawl up into my lap, even though he was nearly as heavy as me. He'd drink his milk, making his cub-like humming noise. His coat was glossy and shiny. It was soft, especially over the top of his head and around his ears. When he stood on his hind legs he came up to my chest. He was strong too, much stronger than he looked. When the tourists came he clamoured for attention, for fruit and nuts. He let people put their hands through the bars to stroke and scratch him and feed him fruits from their hands.

'You see,' said the Doctor to a group of tourists. 'This small cub was orphaned and brought to me. See how strong and healthy he is. See how I have saved him.'

I stood back and watched. I didn't like the Doctor or the tourists feeding him. I didn't like them looking at him, prodding him and poking him or the way they cooed and clucked at him as if he was a small child. They just saw a bear cub. They didn't see the sores on his elbows and back legs from lying on the bars. They didn't see the swollen abdomen of Mama Bear's son, and the way he groaned and grunted with each breath, or the bleeding gums of the bears' mouths where their teeth had been cut short and filed. They saw what they wanted to see, and then they walked away, and they forgot.

I followed the Doctor and the group of tourists to the office where the Doctor sold the bile in bottles, flakes, and powders. It was a big group. Twelve Japanese tourists. Their minibus had pictures of Laos painted along the side, of mountains and golden temples and statues of Buddha. I watched the tourists climb back into their minibus and leave with their bile, a tonic for the way home.

The clouds were low and heavy with more rain yet to come. Cars had their headlights on and the streetlights were lit up, even though it was not yet nightfall. I leant against the door. The Doctor was smiling, counting the notes of money, letting them flip over in his hand. I knocked at the door and he looked up at me.

'The tourists liked the bears today,' he said. 'Here, you have done well.' He pushed a US dollar into the top pocket of my shirt. 'Have this. See how generous I am.'

'Thank you,' I said. I stood, facing him. It was now or never. He was in the best mood I'd seen him in for a long time.

'I was thinking of my family,' I said.

The Doctor looked up.

Moon Bear

'Maybe I could have some time off to visit them,' I said. I started gabbling. 'Just to see Ma and my sisters. It wouldn't be for long.'

The Doctor's face clouded over. He turned away. 'We are very busy here, Mountain Boy.'

'It would be two days at most. Maybe Asang could feed the bears when I am gone.'

The Doctor tapped his fingers on the table. His face creased into a frown. 'Do you have money?'

My hands felt clammy and cold despite the heat. I didn't want him to know I earned some money from Kham's father. 'Maybe I could use a little of the money you send to my mother to pay for my trip home.'

The Doctor took a deep breath in and let it out slowly. 'Do you *know* how much it is to travel home?'

I shook my head.

'Do you *know* how much a bag of rice costs?'

'No,' I said. 'But . . .'

The Doctor looked up sharply. 'Then I suggest that you stay and work so your family can eat.' He stood up, all the smiles gone from him. 'Besides,' he said, snatching up the keys to his motorbike. 'I am going to buy more bears. There will be more work to do here soon.'

I watched the Doctor rev out of the compound, his

wheels spraying grit into the air. I stormed into the bear barn and pulled the sliding doors across, slamming them shut behind me. I flung Sôok-dìi's cage open and he threw his big paws on my shoulders. I shoved him off and walked away. He followed me and tried to snuffle in my pocket for honeyed nuts. I pushed him off again and he loped off to explore beneath the cages of the other bears for food dropped by the tourists. The other bears were quiet, sedated by the drugs and the pressing heat of the day. Above me, raindrops started to patter on the iron roof. The sound seemed to still the bears. Biter raised his head and looked upwards, licking his lips at the sound of water. I slid down against Sôok-dìi's cage and closed my eyes. I thought of the rain in the mountains, thundering on our roofs, turning the smallest streams into mighty rapids. I thought about Ma. Had she managed to plant the rice, or vegetables? Was she even in the same house? It had been so long since I'd seen her.

I thought of Sôok-dìi too. I'd made a promise to him that I would get him back to his home. I couldn't even get back to my own family. How did I think I could get Sôok-dìi back into the forest too? The rain rose from a patter to a steady drumming. Water crept underneath the sliding doors, bringing in bright blood-red mud. The rain hammered against the roof, faster and faster. I couldn't think. I covered my ears and pressed my head into my knees. There was no way out of here. I was as caged as Sôok-dìi and the bears.

The rain stopped as suddenly as it had begun.

It was only then I heard the scream, high pitched and terrified.

'Tam!'

Again the scream.

I looked around. By the sliding doors, I saw Kham splayed on the ground. Sôok-dìi was standing over him, paws pinning his shoulders down, jaws wide open and stretched across Kham's face.

CHAPTER 20

'Sôok-dìi,' I yelled. I ran at him, clapping my hands and flapping my arms in the air. 'Sôok-dìi! Away! Away!'

Sôok-dìi lowered his head and backed off Kham.

'Hup! Hup!' I yelled, still flapping my arms.

Sôok-dìi reared up on his hind legs and took backward steps. I lowered my arms and he slumped on his haunches. I patted the floor and he lay down, his head lowered and ears back. I rummaged in my pocket for his honeyed nuts, scattered them on the floor and spun round to look at Kham.

Kham had crawled backwards and had his back pressed against the sliding doors. A trickle of blood ran down his forehead, from a gash just above his eye. He just stared past me at Sôok-dìi, his mouth hung open.

Moon Bear

I crouched down beside him. 'Kham!'

Still, he stared.

'Kham! Can you hear me?' I shook him by the arm. 'Are you OK?'

He turned to look at me. 'Bear . . .' he said.

'I'm sorry, Kham. I didn't hear you come in . . .'

'Bear . . .' he said again.

'Your face . . . he's drawn blood.'

Kham touched the cut on his head and looked at the fresh blood on his fingers. His eyebrows rose a little in mild surprise.

Sôok-dìi had moved a little closer. He snuffled in my pockets and then started sniffing Kham's feet.

I raised my arms and yelled at him, 'Sit up, Sôok-dìi. Sit. Up.'

Sôok-dìi sat back on his haunches and then slumped on the floor with a groan as if I'd stopped his fun.

I turned to look at Kham again, but he was just staring between the bear and me, a look of utter disbelief on his face.

'It's OK, Kham,' I said. 'I won't let him touch you.'

Kham grabbed my arm and pinned me next to him. 'That bear . . .' he said.

'Let me put him away.' I said the words as slowly and calmly as I could. 'And then I'll take you home.'

Kham pulled me closer still and shook his head. 'No! No! You don't understand.' He turned to me. 'That bear . . .' he said, a huge grin spreading across his face, '. . . that bear is going to earn us a *fortune*.'

I pushed Kham away. 'What?'

Kham scrambled to his feet and pointed at Sôok-dìi. 'He does what you say!'

'So?'

'So . . .' said Kham, '. . . so there hasn't been a dancing bear in the city since the One-Eyed Bear Man's bear ate a tin of rat poison and died.'

'Kham!' I said. It was my turn to pull him round to face me. 'What are you talking about?'

Kham clapped his hands in front of my face and laughed. 'Wake up, Tam! Listen! When I was little, there was a man who used to sit outside the temples and museums and make his bear dance for the tourists. They paid good money to have their photo taken with the bear.'

I frowned. 'So, you saying we take Sôok-dìi into town and let people take photos with him.'

Kham slapped me on the back. 'Exactly.'

Moon Bear

I stretched my foot out and scratched Sôok-dìi behind the ear with my toe. Sôok-dìi rolled over and licked my toes. I thought of the tourists that visited the bile farm, and how they laughed and pointed at the bears. I didn't want that for Sôok-dìi.

'I don't know,' I said. 'Besides . . . I don't know what he's like with strangers. He drew blood on you.'

Kham touched his head. 'He didn't bite me,' he said. 'It's where I hit the ground when he pushed me down.'

I stared at the bump swelling on his head. 'Anyhow, how would we get him into the city centre? We can't just jump on a tuk-tuk with a *bear*.'

Kham stood up and paced up around Sôok-dìi. 'We wouldn't need to. We'd take the three-wheeler and the cart I use to run errands at home. He'd fit in, just.'

I stared at him.

'And . . .' continued Kham, 'we'd be equal partners. We'd split it right down the middle. Fifty-fifty. Half each. I'd get us into the city and collect the money and you'd be in charge of the bear.'

'What if the Doctor finds out?' I said.

Kham rubbed his chin. 'That's the risk you'd have to take,' he said. 'The Doctor is away weekends you say. We'd just go weekends.'

'I'd lose my job,' I said.

'My father said you could work for him.'

I ran my hands through my hair.

Kham opened his hands out. 'Think of the *money*, Tam! What would you do with the money?'

I walked away from him, scuffing the floor with my feet. Sôok-dìi scrambled up and loped along beside me, pushing his nose into my hands. His claws clicked on the concrete. I knelt down and buried my face in his fur. I didn't like the thought of him being gawped at. But maybe Kham was right. If I earned enough I could pay my way to visit home, buy more silks for Ma or food and clothes for Sulee and Mae. The Doctor would never have to know if we only went on the days he was away. Maybe there would even be a way to get Sôok-dìi back to the forest. I paced in circles around his empty cage.

Maybe.

Maybe.

Maybe.

I stared down the line of bears. Hua was sucking at the bars, licking one area over and over. Mama Bear's cub swung side to side, banging his head against his cage. Sôok-dìi leant against me. He was becoming a big bear. In another few months he might be too big to handle. There would soon come a time when the Doctor would milk him for bile. And I would lose him. Sôok-dìi would live like the other bears. Caged. Confined. He would never see the forest, or feel the rain or the earth beneath his feet. He would become a bile bear, and it would be no life at all.

I closed my eyes and tried to push those thoughts away, but an image of him pressed against the bars burned deep in my mind.

Maybe there was no other way.

I walked back to Kham. He was standing with his arms crossed against his chest. 'Well?' he said.

I ran my hands through the fur of Sôok-dìi's head. 'OK, Kham,' I said. 'When do we start?'

Chapter 21

I clung onto Kham's back as he pedalled in and out of the traffic. The early morning sun was bright in our eyes, glaring off car rooftops and windows. The trailer behind his three-wheeler was made from old wooden pallets set on a wheel axle. It was lucky that the road into town was flat, because Sôok-dìi was heavy and he sometimes lurched in the trailer, making it tip. I could hear him scratch and scuffle at the lid and I turned round to see the tip of his nose and paw push against the gaps between the slats. He must have eaten all the melon I'd put in there.

'We'll try one of the small temples near the river first,' Kham yelled back at me. His feet pedalled fast as he pushed out into the centre of the traffic. I could see beads of sweat gather at the nape of his neck and trickle down his shirt.

'It's near the coffee shops and bakeries. There'll be loads of tourists there.'

'I hope it's not far,' I yelled back. 'I don't think Sôok-dìi likes it in there much.'

'It's another five blocks away, but it'll be worth it.'

I held on tight, as cars and lorries and tuk-tuks whizzed past us. I didn't like to even think what would happen if we were knocked over and Sôok-dìi escaped.

'There it is,' said Kham.

The temple's sloping roofs were flame red against the deep blue sky. There were several groups of *falang* standing in the plaza in front.

Kham swung the three-wheeler into an alleyway behind the bakery. The smells of hot sweet bread and coffee rose out in a steam of condensation and mixed with the heady scent of sandalwood from the temple.

Kham leant against the wall, catching his breath. 'Ever had a chocolate croissant?'

I shook my head.

He smiled. 'If we earn enough today, I'll buy you one. You haven't lived if you haven't had one of Madame Philippe's chocolate croissants.'

I looked beyond him to a group of three *falang* sitting at one of the tables beneath the shade of the café's awning. There were two men in T-shirts and shorts. In their twenties, I guessed. Both had beards and shaggy unkempt hair. There was a woman with them too, in a vest top and short skirt. Three huge rucksacks lay at their feet. Ma would have been shocked to see one of the men's feet propped up on the table. I could see the dirt on the soles of his feet.

'Backpackers,' said Kham. He wrinkled his nose. 'Probably English, maybe German. They don't wash so much.'

I watched the woman spread a thick spoonful of jam into her croissant.

Kham leant into me. 'They follow each other like goats. Party goats!' He laughed. 'They say they have no money, but they spend a month's salary in one evening on drink. I don't think we'll get much from them.'

Sôok-dìi scratched again at the trailer. He was getting hot and restless inside. I had no idea what he would be like in the open. I'd made a head collar out of rope, like the ones I'd seen Grandfather make for the buffalo. Grandfather said if you controlled an animal's head, you controlled the whole beast. Sôok-dìi was so strong now, that I knew I'd have little control if he decided to run. I could just about hold him, if he didn't struggle. I fished some more honey-eyed nuts from my pocket and dropped them through the wooden slats.

Moon Bear

Kham nudged me again. 'They're the ones we want to go for.'

I followed his gaze across the road to the red-bricked plaza and gardens in front of the temple. There was a small group of grey-haired *falang* heading towards the temple. They wore pale short-sleeved shirts and long cotton trousers. Each had a camera and small bag. Their white skin was chilli-red where they'd caught the sun.

'Probably Americans,' said Kham. 'They have money. They feel bad about the bombies, so that makes them give more money too.'

I took a deep breath and put my hand out on the trailer. 'They dropped the bombs?'

Kham was staring at me now. 'You heard about them?'

'My father was killed by one,' I said. I rested my head against the trailer. I felt sick and dizzy. Sôok-dìi pushed his nose through the slats and snuffed my hair. His long pink tongue reached through and licked my face.

Kham put his hand on my shoulder. 'I'm sorry,' he said.

I looked up at him.

'I didn't know.' He frowned. 'I thought . . .'

I waited.

Kham pushed his hair back. 'Well, we were told your family had too many children and they couldn't afford to keep you.'

I stared at him. 'Pa died,' I said. 'The Doctor sends my pay back to Ma and my sisters. It's the only way they can keep the house and have somewhere to live.'

Kham just stared at me, as if he was seeing me for the first time.

'Come on,' I said. 'Sôok-dìi will tear this trailer apart if we don't get him out.'

'Do you miss home?'

I thought of Grandfather and Pa, I thought of Ma and my sisters and the forest tracks and our old home high in the mountains. 'Always,' I said.

I reached into my pocket for some honeyed nuts and undid the catch of the lid. Sôok-dìi pushed the lid up with his nose. I slipped the head collar over his head and hauled him out. He stood up on his hind legs, blinking in the strong sunlight, sniffing the air for all the new smells.

He was five months old now, about the same weight as a sack of rice, but one with sharp claws and teeth. He liked to nip at my ankles and I had to bat him away, as I imagined his mother would have done. Kham led me across the road and we sat down on a low wall in the square

Moon Bear

opposite the temple. I could see people looking our way.

Sôok-dìi pressed against me, his eyes wide, watching all the different people. He scrambled onto my lap and clung around my neck, humming quietly in my ear.

'It's all right,' I said. 'It's OK.'

Kham nudged me. 'Make him dance.'

'He can't,' I said.

'Go on, make him stand up and walk about.'

I stood up and pulled some cane toffee from my pocket. 'Hup, Sôok-dìi,' I said. 'Hup.'

Sôok-dìi rose up on his hind legs. I took steps backwards holding the toffee in my hand. Sôok-dìi took steps towards me, flapping his paws. His round ears pricked forward, he stuck out his long tongue, trying to reach the toffee.

When I turned round, I saw a small crowd had gathered behind us. Some people had their cameras out and were taking photos and filming. Kham stood in front of me.

'A dollar for a photo with the bear,' Kham called. 'Have your photo with a bear cub.'

One lady stepped forward. She pressed some notes into Kham's hand and came to stand beside me. I watched Sôok-dìi. I didn't know what he would do. He'd never had a stranger this close before. If he bit her, we were in deep trouble. I handed her a piece of cane toffee for her to feed. She wrapped her arm around Sôok-dìi and fed the toffee while her husband snapped away with his camera. Sôok-dìi snuffled in her hand and tugged at her sleeves and the leather strap to her bag.

'Any more?' said Kham, to the gathering crowd, ushering the lady away. 'Anyone else want a photo with the bear?'

'Thirty dollars!' said Kham. 'Real US dollars!'

We sat on the concrete floor of the bear barn. Sôok-dìi was asleep, his big head resting in my lap. He twitched and licked his lips in his dreams.

Kham held a bag with two chocolate croissants in his hand, but he couldn't stop staring at the money. 'It's true what they said about Sôok-dìi. He'll bring us good fortune.'

'Half each, you said,' I reminded him.

Kham nodded. He started counting out the money into two piles.

'And some for Sôok-dìi,' I said.

Kham looked up. 'For Sôok-dìi?'

'For his cane toffee and honeyed nuts. He won't listen to me unless he has his toffee.'

Moon Bear

Kham nodded. 'I guess it's only fair.' He counted out notes in a separate pile. 'Cane toffee money,' he said.

I picked up my pile of notes. I'd never owned so much before.

'What will you do with it?' said Kham.

I flipped the notes in my hands. 'Take it home. I'll keep it and take it home to Ma.' I thought of the silks I could buy. Maybe my sisters could go to school. I'd be able to go back to the village and visit them. 'What about you?' I said.

Kham rolled the notes and slipped them in his pocket. 'I'll use it to make more money.' He laughed. 'That's what you do with money. You use it to make more.'

I yawned and stretched my legs out in front of me. I took a bite of the end of the croissant and chewed it slowly.

'Next Saturday,' said Kham. 'We'll do it again.'

OK,' I said. I yawned again.

Kham took a bite of his croissant. 'D'you like it?'

I nodded and took another bite.

Kham wiped chocolate from around his mouth. 'My father says the cakes and pastries are the best things the French ever did for Laos.'

My mouth was full of warm sweet bread and the flakes of croissant were scattered on my chest. Sôok-dii woke up and nuzzled into me looking for crumbs.

Kham rubbed his nose. 'You know, we'd earn more money if you taught Sôok-dìi a few tricks.'

'Like what?'

'I don't know. Maybe he could dance to music? Maybe you could get him to jump through hoops.'

I frowned. 'He doesn't want to dance for his money. He's not that sort of bear.'

'Oh come on, Tam, he enjoyed it today.'

'He enjoyed the cane toffee,' I said.

'Everyone loved him,' said Kham. He pinched my cheek. 'They loved you too.'

I scowled at him.

'It's true. The Americans especially loved you. The lady with the big hair gave double.'

'Just leave it,' I snapped. 'I'm only doing it to get back home.'

Kham chewed on the last mouthful of his croissant and watched me. 'I'm sorry about your Pa, really, I am.' He gave a half smile. 'But you know, if you'd lost and arm or leg yourself from the bombies, that American would have paid you even more money. Guilt money. Maybe we could strap up your leg or something?'

I stood up and heaved Sôok-dìi in his cage.

Moon Bear

Kham got up to leave. He slapped me on the shoulder. 'Don't tell me,' he said. 'You're not that sort of boy.'

That night I lay on my mattress and stared through the high window. The sky outside had darkened. I didn't want to switch the light on. I didn't want anyone to see the money I had in my hand. Only Kham knew about the money and I knew he wouldn't tell. His ma would stop him if she discovered his new money making scheme.

I couldn't hide the money under the bed or keep it on me. I opened the small cupboard and brought out the empty honey tin. I opened the lid and pushed the notes inside. I stood on the table and reached up to wedge the tin between the brickwork and the metal of the corrugated iron roof. It couldn't be seen from the ground. Someone would have to search the room to find it. It was the safest place for now.

I lay back down and looked up at the rising crescent moon. I could hardly bring myself to think about it, but hope rose up inside me too. I wanted to believe it, for Sôok-dìi and for me. I wanted to believe there really was a way I could get us both back home again.

CHAPTER 22

I was sweeping the yard when General Chan's car swept in to the bear farm. He stepped out and brushed the creases from his trousers. 'I have come for more bile.'

I glanced around, half expecting the Doctor to appear. 'The Doctor is not here yet, but I can get you some bile from the office.'

General Chan's eyes rested on me for a moment. He looked at his watch. 'When will he be here?'

'Soon,' I said. 'Soon.'

The mid-morning sun was hot. A line of sweat trickled down General Chan's face.

'Would you like to wait in the office?' I said.

General Chan turned away from me. 'I will wait in the car.' The driver opened the car door for him and I felt a blast of ice cool air in my face. I could see two people in the back, a boy and a girl, both older than me.

General Chan climbed in and the driver shut the door, leaving the engine running.

I walked back to the bear barn. I'd cleaned beneath the cages and sprayed the bears with water. I hadn't fed them as the Doctor said they produced more bile if they were starved.

I hated this time, knowing the Doctor would arrive soon. I felt the fear run through me. I felt it in the bears' pacing and restlessness. I paced with them, up and down the central aisle, counting the drainage grilles. One, two, three, four . . . turn . . . one, two, three, four . . . turn. The bears watched me. Sôok-dìi pushed his paw through the bars and tried to pat me as I passed.

One, two, three, four . . .

Turn.

One, two . . .

'Hello!'

I looked up. I hadn't heard anyone enter the barn. The girl and boy from the car were silhouetted against the brightness of the open door.

The girl stepped forward. 'Hello, I'm Savanh.'

I stared at her.

I guessed she was sixteen, maybe seventeen. She was small for her age. Thin too. She wore jeans and a white T-shirt. A silk scarf was wrapped around her head and fell down the back of her neck like golden hair. Her skin was the colour of the rice moon. If this was General Chan's daughter, then it was true. She was beautiful. Too beautiful, Ma would have said. Maybe she was sick because the spirits saw her from their heavens and wanted her back.

She took another step towards me. 'I wonder if we could see the bears.'

I looked around. I couldn't see General Chan. I guessed he was waiting in the car.

The boy took a step into the barn too. He looked slightly older than Savanh. He wore jeans too, and a leather jacket. His dark hair stood in sharp spikes on his head. He pushed his sunglasses up and looked around.

'This is my friend, Talin,' said Savanh.

Talin didn't look at me. He wrinkled his nose and turned to Savanh. 'You don't want to do this, do you?'

Savanh turned to me and smiled. 'Can we?' she said. 'Can we see the bears?'

I nodded. 'Watch him, though.' I pointed at Biter. 'Don't put your hand through the bars.'

I watched Savanh and Talin wander down the aisle.

Moon Bear

Talin kept checking his shoes, turning them over to see if there was any dirt on the soles of his bright white trainers. He wrinkled his nose and looked at his watch. 'How long do we have to wait?'

Savanh stopped at Mama Bear's son's cage and turned to me. 'My father has a small zoo,' she said. 'He rescues orphaned animals from the forest. We have birds and gibbons and deer, and even a golden cat.' She smiled. 'Jean-Paul is still my favourite.'

'Jean-Paul?' I said.

'Jean-Paul is an old, old tiger. He has no teeth.' She watched Mama Bear's son sway side to side. 'Jean-Paul likes to pace up and down his enclosure. Up and down. Up and down. He paces so much, his feet carve deep trenches in the earth.'

Talin walked away from us, staring into the cages.

'I always felt sorry for Jean-Paul,' said Savanh. 'I always thought he wanted freedom.' She smiled and looked at me. 'But you know, one day, the gardener left his cage door wide, wide open. He didn't try to escape. He just kept on pacing up and down beside the open door.' She laughed. 'My father says Jean-Paul likes the thought of freedom, but is too scared to take it. It is too easy being fed and watered in a cage.'

I just stared at Mama Bear's son rocking backwards and forwards.

'What do you think?' she asked me. 'Do you think he wants his freedom?'

I shrugged my shoulders. 'Maybe he doesn't know where to find it.'

Savanh turned round to look at me. She opened her mouth as if she was about to say something but turned back to the bears. She walked along the row, passing Jem and Jep, coming to stop at Biter's cage. 'How do you take them to their outdoor enclosures?'

'What d'you mean?' I said.

'Where they can stretch and play. We have a sun bear and he has a garden with a pond to bathe in.'

I stared at Biter pressed against the bars. 'This is it,' I said. 'This is where they stay.'

Savanh turned to me, eyes wide open. 'Always?'

'Always,' I said.

Savanh stared along the line of bears. 'I didn't think it would be like this.'

I walked away from her and she followed me to Sôok-dìi's cage. He snuffed the air and stretched his paws through the bars.

Talin stood looking in, careful not to let his jacket

touch the bars.

Savanh's face broke into a big smile. 'This one's just a baby.'

'He's five months old,' I said.

Savanh reached in and scratched his ear. 'Look, Talin, he's very friendly.'

Talin stepped between us. He was staring at me, looking me up and down. 'I heard there were two boys and a dancing bear cub in town last week, outside Philippe's. Dancing for the *falang*.'

My mouth went dry. I stared hard at the metal bars, tracing the patterns of red rust with my finger.

Talin leaned closer. 'Wouldn't be you, would it?'

My breaths came short and shallow. 'These are bile bears,' I said. 'Not dancing bears.'

Savanh looked between Talin and me. She laughed and nudged him in the side. 'You like dancing, Talin. Maybe you could join them.'

Talin scowled and flipped his sunglasses back over his eyes. I couldn't tell if he was looking at me or not. Maybe that's what he wanted. 'Look, Savanh,' he said. 'Here comes your father.'

Savanh looked beyond me to see her father, Asang, and the Doctor walking towards us.

Mama Bear's son hooted and pressed against the furthest space of his cage. The other bears moaned and shuffled.

Savanh took my arm. 'What's his name?' she said.

I turned to look at her. 'Who?'

'The bear cub! What's his name?'

'Sôok-dìi,' I said.

Savanh reached through and ran her hands across the fur on Sôok-dìi's back. I watched her eyes trace an arc from the bare bars of the cage to the hard concrete floor beneath. She ran her hand to the softest fur behind his ears. She bent close down. 'Sôok-dìi,' she whispered. 'I wish you all the luck in the world.'

I swept the yard after Savanh and her father and her friend had left. General Chan had wanted fresh bile for Savanh. I'd heard him tell the Doctor that she was getting sick again. Her doctors had made a special paste of herbs and lime juice to mix with the bile. She had to drink it straight from the bear, they said.

I swept up and down, past the wide, open gates. Up and down. Up and down. Every time I passed the gates, I thought of Jean-Paul. He chose not to take his freedom.

Moon Bear

Why? Was he scared? Was freedom just an idea, a thought, a feeling? Maybe he didn't even know what freedom was. I'm sure Biter did. Biter paced the mountains of his mind. The dark forests burned deep within in his eyes. But what about Mama Bear's son, born behind bars? Was freedom just some deep restlessness inside? I thought of the wild pigs and the wild deer and how our ancestors had caught them and bred the freedom from them. The village pigs and buffalo didn't want to escape. Their cages and corrals became their safety. Maybe it could happen with people too. Maybe that's what Grandfather meant when he said we'd sold our freedom.

I thought that maybe I should make my escape soon, before I too might forget.

CHAPTER 23

After another month, Kham and I had worked out our routine. We'd leave early with Sôok-dìi and cycle to our chosen site. We changed it all the time, in case Savanh's friend saw us there. Philippe's was always the most successful. The tourists liked to eat in the bars and bistros and watch us perform in the square across the road.

I'd taught Sôok-dìi new tricks too. Kham persuaded me to dress Sôok-dìi in clothes. I hated it, but the tourists seemed to love it. Kham bought a lady's dress and scarf to dress Sôok-dìi. Sôok-dìi even allowed me to put a pair of sunglasses on his head. He would reach out his lips and tongue and try to take the peanuts from my hand.

'OK,' said Kham, 'let's do Philippe's today. There's a festival. The city centre will be heaving.'

Moon Bear

I ran along beside him. Sôok-dìi had grown a lot in the last month. He was nearly six months old now and he was discovering he could use his weight to push me around. I wondered how much longer we'd be able to take him into town.

Kham pulled up in the alley behind Philippe's. Madame Philippe saw us and brought us chocolate and almond croissants, warm and sticky from the oven.

She pushed a baguette crust through the wooden crate for Sôok-dìi. 'So you come to us today?'

Kham grinned. 'It's our favourite place.'

Madame Philippe leant against the wall and lit a cigarette. She was older than old. She had white hair, wide-set eyes and the big nose of a *falang*. She always wore long colourful dresses and silk scarves, and bright red lipstick. Kham said her grandfather had been a French diplomat and she thought of herself as French. Sometimes she only spoke in French all day. Today was an exception.

'You should come here every day,' she said. 'Word gets around. The *falang* want to see Madame Philippe's dancing bear.'

Kham took another bite of croissant. 'Wait till you see our new show.' He grinned and nudged me. 'Go on, Tam, you tell her.'

I shook my head and picked almonds from my croissant.

Kham leant close to her. 'Today you will see for the first time, the French lady at the bar!'

Madame Philippe took a deep puff and exhaled, letting out a steady flow of smoke through her nostrils. 'Oh yes?'

Kham nodded. 'Look here. These belong to the bear.' He opened a shoulder bag. 'Maybe we could borrow a table and chair for our French lady.'

Madame Philippe peered in the bag then threw back her head and laughed. 'This, I can't wait to see.'

Kham and I waited until more tourists had gathered in the square. I bought Sôok-dìi a bag with frozen orange juice, pulled off the wrapping and let him suck on the block of sugared ice. He held it in his paws licking it and scrunched at the ice with his front teeth.

'Look,' said Kham. 'A coachload of tourists.'

He grabbed a plastic table and chair from Philippe's and we guided Sôok-dìi through the traffic. I had the head collar tight around his head, but still he wanted to pull me back to Philippe's to the smells of sugar and bread.

The *falang* were spilling out of the coach and swarming into the square. Some of them started taking

Moon Bear

photos of the temple, but I noticed others were pointing at Sôok-dìi.

Kham set the chair and table in the centre of the square and put his brother's CD player on the ground. French café music filled the air around us with the strange sounds of foreign instruments and a woman's voice.

'She sounds like a strangled chicken,' I said.

Kham leant into me. 'It's Edith Piaf, famous French lady, Madame Philippe's favourite.' The *falang* spread around us in a semi-circle. I clapped my hands for Sôok-dìi to stand up. He reared on his hind legs, flapping his front paws, while I opened the shoulder bag and laid out clothes on the ground.

Sôok-dìi dropped onto his forepaws to nose the clothes and brought each item to me. Each time I rewarded him with honeyed peanuts. We'd kept him hungry so he would be keen to do the tricks. I wrapped each piece of clothing around him; a dress, a scarf and then a big floppy hat. He let me put them on, draping the scarf around his neck. He even pulled it across with his mouth.

I hated making him dress like this. It was Kham's idea. He said the One-Eyed Bear Man's bear dressed as a king while the Bear Man got him to dance to his tune.

Out of the corner of my eye, I could see more people,

not just *falang* but locals too. They all wanted to see what the bear could do.

'Hup,' I said when Sôok-dìi was fully dressed in floating dress and floppy hat. People laughed and took photos while Kham walked around them collecting money in his hat. I tried to ignore them, tried to concentrate on the trick. Sôok-dìi followed me to the table and chair. I patted the chair for him to climb on. He climbed up but the chair tipped backwards, and he tumbled over his head, his dress flying above his head, showing his backside in the air. He scratched his bottom and people howled with laughter and clapped. Sôok-dìi didn't seem concerned. I put the chair up and he climbed on, nuzzling in my hand for peanuts. He sat there, a well-dressed French bear. A French lady-bear.

I went to the second part of the act and threw a cloth across the table. Sôok-dìi patted the cloth with his paw and hooted, and again people laughed. I let him snuffle the peanut from my hand, and then I put a plastic bottle on the table and pretended to pour a glass, but Sôok-dìi took the bottle from me and held it like the milk bottle I had given him when he was small. He guzzled the sweet orange juice inside.

People clapped and cheered. I could hear Kham calling

them over for a photo. Some took photos and many threw more money into our hat. Sôok-dìi was bored now there was no food. I could see him trying to pull the clothes off. He tugged the dress and I heard a rip.

Kham nudged me. 'Look, another coach party. We'll be rich today.'

'No,' I said. 'He's done enough.' I pulled the clothes from Sôok-dìi and he tried to claw the paper packet of nuts from my pocket.

'Just one more,' said Kham.

'No, he's done for today.'

Kham picked up the hat and glared at me, but I took Sôok-dìi by the head collar and led him back across the street.

Madame Philippe waved at us. 'Stay,' she called. 'Our customers want more.'

I kept walking across the street to the alley where we parked the bike and cart. I looked back to see Kham take the table and chairs back and talk to Madame Philippe. I heaved Sôok-dìi into the trailer throwing honeyed nuts to lure him in. I buried my head in his soft fur.

Sôok-dìi nuzzled my hand and snuffed my hair.

I closed the lid on him as a shadow fell across the crate. 'Kham . . . ' I said.

I turned.

But it wasn't Kham.

It was someone else.

I could hardly speak.

'What are *you* doing here?'

CHAPTER 24

'Noy!'

Noy stared back at me. He seemed taller than I remembered. He looked so different in a white T-shirt, faded jeans and trainers.

'Noy, what are you doing here?'

Noy walked around the trailer. 'So, this is what you are doing now.'

'Well, not just this,' I said.

Noy leant against the seat of the bicycle. He folded his arms and glared at me. 'A bit of a shock seeing me, is it?'

I took a step towards him. 'Noy!' I smiled and held my arms out. 'I just didn't expect to see you here.'

Noy spat on the ground. 'Neither did I. Last we heard, you were in Thailand.'

'What?' I said.

'Thailand,' said Noy. 'When the money didn't arrive, we were told you'd left your job and disappeared to Thailand.'

I felt sick. 'When the money didn't arrive?'

Noy narrowed his eyes at me. 'Don't pretend you don't know.'

'Noy!' I almost shouted at him. 'What do you mean?'

Noy stood up and paced around me. 'Your ma received one payment and then we were told you'd gone.'

'One payment?' I pressed my head against the crate. 'Are you sure?'

'It's not been easy for her, Tam. Or for any of us.'

I looked at Noy, but his face was hard stone.

'You left us, Tam,' he said. His face darkened. He looked like a boy again. 'You left *me*.'

'I had no choice, Noy.' I was shouting now. 'But I haven't stopped working. I've been at the same farm, the bear farm. My boss, the Doctor, said he'd sent the money home.'

Noy turned to the sound of splintering of wood as Sôok-dìi tried to claw his way out.

I repeated the words as the truth sank deep inside me. '*The Doctor said he'd sent the money home.*'

Moon Bear

'Tam?'

I turned. Kham was standing behind me, a bag of croissants in one hand and the hat bulging with the money in the other.

He looked between Noy and me.

'This is Noy,' I said. 'A friend from home.'

Noy glared back at me.

We didn't look much like old friends.

Kham tightened his grip on the hat.

'Noy, you have to believe me. I've worked every day. Every day.' I turned to Kham. 'Tell him, Kham.'

Kham took a back step.

I grabbed the hat from Kham before he could stop me, and opened it in front of Noy. 'Look!' I said. 'Look!' A thick wodge of notes filled the hat, weighed down by coins.

Noy's eyes widened.

'That's what I'm taking home, to Ma and Mae and Sulee.'

Noy frowned.

'They are OK?' I pulled on his arm. 'Tell me they're OK?'

Noy pulled away. 'They are well. Mae was lucky. She pulled through the sickness.'

'What sickness?

Noy's mouth curled downwards. 'Not long after you left, a sickness came with the rains.'

I said nothing. A breeze blew a plastic bag. It scuttled past, along the sides of the alleyway.

'Four died,' said Noy. 'My father was one of them.'

'Your father? Noy, I'm so sorry.' I wanted to reach out to him, but Noy just glared at me. 'But who is our chief now?' I said.

Noy let out a short laugh. 'My brother. Who did you think? My father's pig would do a better job.'

'Tam,' Kham nudged me in the ribs. 'We must go. See, Sôok-dìi is getting restless.'

Sôok-dìi had worked one of the wooden slats free while we were talking.

I held the money in Noy's face. 'Come back to the village with me. Come back with me and we'll bring this money with us. I have more. I have more to bring.'

Kham snatched the money hat and shoved it in the shoulder bag. He swung his leg over the bicycle and spun the pedal round, ready to be off. 'Come on, Tam.'

I climbed up beside him and wrapped my arms around his waist.

I turned to Noy. 'How will I find you?'

Noy backed away.

Moon Bear

'Where are you staying?' I called.

'With friends,' he said.

'What friends?'

'I have friends, here, in the city,' said Noy. 'I work for them.'

Kham pushed the pedal down and the bicycle lurched forward.

'Find me,' I yelled. 'Come to Sone Motors and find me.'

Kham pedalled out into the bright sunlight of the street. I looked back, but I couldn't see Noy. He was hidden from me, hidden deep within the shadows of the alley.

I sat cross-legged on the cool concrete of the bear barn. Sôok-dìi was stretched out in his cage. Water dripped from his fur where I'd hosed him down.

Kham put the hat with the money on the floor between us.

'It looks like the most we've ever earned,' I said.

Kham tipped it out, the coins raining on the concrete. 'Your friend was very interested in the money,' he said.

'He's saving for his family.'

Kham shrugged. 'He didn't say that.'

I glared at him. 'He didn't have to. He's going to make money and take it home.'

Kham started counting out the money in two piles. 'Did he say what he was doing or where he was staying?'

No,' I said. I felt hot and sticky. Kham's questions crawled like ants across my skin. 'Why should he?'

Kham stopped counting. 'Look, Tam,' he sighed. 'There's bad stuff in the city. Bad people too. And some people who come here become lost. They lose themselves.'

'Noy's not like that,' I said. 'He's my friend. He's family.'

Kham resumed counting. I just stared at the money piling in front of us. The bears snuffled. High above a lone bird fluttered against the tin roof trying to find a way out.

'Ninety-six dollars,' he said, counting out the last few notes. 'We'll be rich on this.'

'The Doctor lied to me,' I said.

Kham continued counting. 'If we'd stayed at Philippe's longer, we could have earned double.'

'He lied,' I said. 'He said he'd send money home, but he lied.'

Kham sighed and sat back and looked at me. 'So, what are you going to do about it?'

Moon Bear

I ran my hands through my hair and stared upwards. The bird threw itself again and again at the roof. I wished it would find its way out. I said nothing. I knew there would be nothing I could say or do to make the Doctor give back the money he owed.

But I knew what I was going to do. I was going to get Sôok-dìi out of here. But first there was something else I needed to do, something I needed Kham to help me with.

'I need to take this money home,' I said.

Kham nodded and pushed one pile of money towards me.

'I'm taking the money I have to Ma.'

Kham put his share back in the hat.

'I could go next weekend,' I said. 'I could take a riverboat on Friday and come back Sunday. Two days. That's all. The Doctor wouldn't know.'

Kham fiddled with the edges of the hat.

'But there would be no one to feed the bears,' I said.

Kham got up to leave.

'Kham?' I said.

Kham turned to me. 'OK, Tam. Just this once. Just this once I will feed the bears.'

'Really? You'd do that?'

'Just food and water,' he said. 'I'm not cleaning them.'

'Thank you, Kham,' I said. I wanted to hug him. 'Thank you.'

I took my share of the money and we each counted out some notes for Sôok-dìi's treats.

Kham counted extra notes for Sôok-dìi. 'Put more for him,' he said. 'He needs a pay rise.'

'A pay rise?'

'Didn't you see how the *falang* loved our lady-bear today?'

I laughed. Although I hated seeing Sôok-dìi dressed up, he had drawn in the crowds. They couldn't get enough of him.

'So,' said Kham, 'he needs accessories . . . a little handbag, a necklace. Maybe some lipstick!'

'Lipstick?'

'Oh yes,' said Kham with a wicked smile. 'Think of the money. A dollar for a photo with the bear, ten dollars for a kiss.'

CHAPTER 25

I couldn't concentrate on anything all week. I wanted so much to go home, to see Ma, to see my family. I bought more silks for Ma and a dress each for Mae and Sulee. I folded the rest of the money in the honey tin and kept it safe, high in the crack between the corrugated iron roof and the wall. The tin was packed full with money. I'd never earned so much before. It could buy Ma rice and chickens, maybe even a buffalo. I hadn't asked Noy if Ma still had the house or the land we'd been given. Maybe we could even buy some fruit trees and hives and keep bees like Pa wanted us to. I didn't know how much to keep back for Sôok-dìi, but I knew Ma needed the money more. I'd save up again for money to get Sôok-dìi back into the forests.

'Mountain Boy!' The Doctor clapped his hands in front of my face. 'Wake up!'

I jolted from my daydream. The hosepipe in my hand was dribbling a steady trickle of water on the floor. I started hosing the floors, spraying water beneath the cages.

'This place must be clean for General Chan and his daughter.' He rubbed his hands together. 'My bears are getting a reputation as the bears to cure all ills.'

As much as I hated the milking days, I looked forward to seeing Savanh. She had come each week with her father to drink the fresh bile from Biter. She'd tell me I should learn to read. If we were alone, waiting for Biter's sedation, she'd even try to teach me, dipping her finger in water and tracing Lao script on the dry concrete. I'd watch the dark patterns form and disappear as the words dried up in the heat. Even the bears seemed calmer with Savanh there.

I heard General Chan's car pull up in the yard and watched as the Doctor hauled open the sliding doors. But neither the General nor Savanh was in the car. The driver opened the back door and Savanh's friend, Talin, stepped out.

He walked up to the Doctor. 'General Chan's daughter is too sick to come today,' he said.

Moon Bear

The Doctor studied Talin's face. 'Please send his daughter my best wishes.'

Talin pushed his sunglasses up on his head. 'The General says that he would like to see you next week. He does not think your bears are of the top quality and he may look elsewhere.'

The Doctor smiled through his teeth. 'These are the best bears, I can assure him.'

'Well,' said Talin. 'General Chan is not convinced. He would like me to buy some fresh bile today, but he will see you next week.'

'Yes, of course,' said the Doctor bowing and backing away. 'Of course.'

Talin waited in the office while we milked Biter. The Doctor was rougher with Biter today. He hauled him from his cage. He jabbed hard to find the bile and left him sore and bleeding. The Doctor's jaw muscles clenched and un-clenched as he worked.

The Doctor swirled Biter's bile in the glass flask and held it up to the light. It was a dark brown greenish sludge, tinged with blood. 'Here, Mountain Boy. Give this to Talin. Tell him that this is free today.'

I nodded and took the bile. I found Talin in the of-fice. He was sitting back in the chair, a bored expression on his face. I emptied the flask into little glass vials and gave them to him.

'This is for General Chan,' I said. 'The Doctor says there is no charge today.'

He took the vials without a word.

'Please,' I said, as he took a first step outside.

He turned.

I stared at my feet. 'Please can you say hello from me to Savanh.'

Talin snorted a laugh.

I felt my face burn.

'Savanh has more on her mind than listening to well wishes from a cleaning boy,' he said.

I watched him climb in the car and leave. It slid out of the yard into the traffic of the road and disappeared. I glanced back at the Doctor. So Savanh was sick again and General Chan wasn't pleased. The Doctor's bears weren't so special after all.

It was hard leaving Sôok-dìi that night, knowing I wouldn't see him for another two days. I knew Kham wouldn't want to let him out, so I let Sôok-dìi play in the barn for longer. I let him play his favourite game of melon football, chasing a melon around the barn. I did wonder if I could take him with me. But could I take a bear on board the riverboat? Where would I keep him at the village?

I put him back in his cage and scratched behind his ear. 'I'll come back for you,' I said. 'Maybe I could find us a riverboat to the forests.'

Sôok-dìi held my hand in his paws as if he was listening.

I pressed my head against his. 'That's what we'll do, Sôok-dìi. When I come back from seeing Ma and Mae and Sulee, I'll take you away from here. We'll escape. I'll take you back, to the forests.'

'Tam?'

I turned.

Kham was standing in the gap of the barn doors. 'Who are you talking to in there?'

I closed Sôok-dìi's cage. 'No one,' I said.

Kham glanced back over his shoulder. 'Your friend wants to see you,' he said, 'the one from your home.'

I jumped up. 'Noy? Noy is here now?'

Kham frowned. 'Tam, listen . . . '

'Noy is here!' I said. I pushed past Kham to see Noy standing by the gates, lit by streetlight. 'Noy!' I shouted and waved.

I crossed the road to him. Noy was leaning against the fence, his hands deep in his pockets, but he was smiling.

'Noy!' I said. I couldn't take my eyes from him. 'You found me.'

Noy grinned.

'You're not mad at me still?'

'No,' said Noy.

'Come,' I said. I led him towards the yellow light of my room.

'Tam!' Kham backed away towards his house. 'My father is shutting the gates soon. Your friend cannot stay long.'

Noy looked around the room, taking in the thin mattress, the low table and the chest of drawers. 'I thought it was true that you'd gone and left. I didn't realize you'd been working all this time.'

'And I didn't realize my boss hadn't been sending the money,' I said.

Noy paced around the room, fiddling with the drawers and poking behind the clothes and peanut treats on my shelves. 'You must earn a bit with the dancing bear,' he said.

'More than just a bit,' I said.

Noy lifted up a packet of silks and pulled out a few golden threads. He whistled softly. 'This must have been expensive.'

'It was,' I said. 'I'm taking it back to Ma.'

Noy frowned. 'You spent it all on silks?'

'No,' I laughed. 'There's more. Loads more. Enough to buy a buffalo.'

Noy put down the silks and looked at me. 'Let's see.'

'It's safe,' I said. Something stopped me from telling him where I'd put the money. I could trust Noy, I'd known him all my life, but this money for Ma was so precious I didn't want to show anyone.

Noy shrugged his shoulders and slumped on the mattress.

I lay down next to him and we turned on our backs, looking up at the bare light bulb as if it was the moon we'd shared our secrets with before. 'You haven't told me what you do here in the city,' I said.

'Me?' said Noy. 'I carry things.'

'What things?'

'Parcels . . . that sort of stuff.'

'Who for?'

Noy sat up. 'Why the questions, Tam?'

'Do you earn enough money?'

Noy pulled back his sleeve to show a huge gold watch on his wrist. 'See, my boss is very generous. He gave this to me.'

I stared at the watch. I couldn't tell if it was real gold, but it looked expensive.

'I'm going back,' I said, 'to the village.'

Noy turned to look at me. 'It's not the same,' he said. 'There are new people, from other villages.' He frowned. 'It's not the same.'

'What about your TV? Did you get to watch it?'

'It's my brother's TV now.' Noy laughed. 'There *is* electricity, but we can't afford it.'

We lay in silence, listening to the buzz of the electric light above our heads and the sounds of the traffic on the road outside.

'You know the bear cub?' I said.

Noy frowned. 'What cub?'

'The cub we tried to take from the den?' I said. 'Well it's the bear here at the farm, the dancing bear.'

Noy turned to look at me. 'Is that so?' he said. He gave a short laugh. 'The three of us ended up in the city to find our fortune.'

I smiled. 'I didn't tell you, but I was terrified that night. I thought the mother bear was going to kill me.'

Noy's face broke into a grin. 'I thought so too.'

'D'you miss our old home in the forest?' I said.

Noy didn't answer.

Moon Bear

I smiled. 'Remember when we thought we were so big and clever for making a rope bridge across the fast river?'

Noy nodded. 'We got in whole load of trouble for that, didn't we? Ma said we could have drowned.'

I laughed. 'Grandfather taught me how to tie good knots after that.'

Noy put his hands beneath his head and stared up at the ceiling. He drew in a deep breath and let it out slowly. 'It was simple back then, wasn't it? It was good. I don't know why I couldn't see it.'

'Come back with me,' I said.

Noy looked at me.

'Come back with me to the village. I'm going tomorrow. I'm catching a slow boat at dawn and taking Ma the money. I'm going back.'

Noy stared at his watch and turned it round and round his wrist, watching the gold strap catch the light.

'Noy,' I said, 'the village needs us both. Maybe it could be like old times.'

He pushed his sleeve over his wrist and looked at me and smiled. 'OK,' he said. 'Maybe you're right. Maybe it is time we both went back home.'

CHAPTER 26

The river was busy at first light. The sun's rim broke above the distant hills, igniting the sky and casting the ground in deep chocolate shadow. Monks walked along the riverside, their saffron robes the colour of the dawn-reflected Mekong. The rich scent of coffee and spice and sandalwood mixed together, a sweet heady mix in the still air.

There were already queues for the riverboats. The rains had swollen the Mekong. The river ran fast, churning currents from deep below. Kham had warned that sometimes the boats could not run in full flood. I hoped I'd be able to board a boat today.

I stood at the river's edge and closed my eyes. The chanting of the monks soothed me. It made it seem possible that soon I would see Ma and Mae and Sulee. I held the shoulder bag I'd borrowed from Kham tight against me. It was packed full of the silks and threads and presents for back home. I felt for the hard edges of the money-filled honey-tin inside the bag. I thought of Ma's face seeing the money. I thought of all the things we could use it for.

'Hey, Tam.'

I opened my eyes and turned. Noy was walking towards me. I smiled and waved. Part of me had wondered whether he'd really come today. But now we would return together, as it should be.

'Have you got the tickets?' he said.

I shook my head. 'Which boat?' I said. They all looked the same to me.

'Come,' said Noy.

I followed him, weaving around stalls and people with bags and cages and woven baskets of rice. My stomach growled. I hadn't eaten and I was starving. Noy spoke to several of the boatmen. Some of the boats were already full.

'Tam,' said Noy, 'stand in this queue and I'll get the tickets.'

I stopped beside a woman with a basket of chickens and a bicycle wheel.

Noy held out his hand. 'I need some money,' he said, 'for the tickets.'

I opened my shoulder bag and pulled the tin to the top of the bag. 'How much for the tickets?' I said.

Noy looked around him. 'I'll take the tin,' he said.

I shook my head. 'I don't want people seeing how much there is.' I pulled out some notes and handed them to him. 'This should be enough.'

Noy took the money and disappeared through the crowd. I stood in the queue clutching my bag to me.

Our riverboat was an open-sided longboat, painted red and green. Her low flat roof reflected the gold of the sky. I could see the captain, a small skinny man in a T-shirt, shorts, and a peaked cap. He was busy with the engine. Puffs of thick black smoke belched out from the back of the boat. Another crew member pushed a long thin plank from the boat to the riverbank and beckoned us to board. I looked around for Noy and saw him pushing his way through. He shoved a ticket in my hand. 'It's a return ticket,' he said. 'Keep it safe.'

We inched forward. I could see the boat filling up in front of us. One crew member was slinging bags and luggage across to another while the passengers edged across the thin plank. The crewman threw my bag across and Noy went first. I watched the plank bow and bend beneath his weight.

Moon Bear

Noy picked up my bag and turned to face me. 'I'll find a seat for us,' he yelled, and disappeared beneath the low roof of the boat.

I edged my way across the thin plank, keeping my eyes fixed on my feet. Below, the yellow waters of the Mekong swept beneath me. If I fell, I'd be pulled beneath the line of boats moored along the riverbanks. I would stand no chance. I climbed into the boat and squeezed my way through people and bags and cages and baskets. I couldn't see Noy at first, then I saw him at the front on one of the hard seats, his arm safe around my bag. He waved for me to join him. I scrambled over cages of chickens and sat down beside him, taking my bag from him. I held it close, feeling the hard edge of the honey-tin against my chest.

I looked at Noy, but he was frowning, looking out to market stalls and vendors lined up along the riverbank. His leg jiggled against mine.

'Nervous?' I asked.

Noy jumped.

'I am too,' I said. 'It'll be strange going back.'

He looked at me and a brief smile broke along his face. 'A bit,' he said. 'My brother and I didn't leave on good terms.'

'He'll understand,' I said. 'I bet he's missing you.'

But Noy wasn't listening. His eyes scanned the market. 'Are you hungry?'

'Starving,' I said.

Noy jumped up. 'I'll get us some food and drink. It's a long trip.'

I pulled him down. 'The boat's about to leave.'

Noy pulled away. 'I won't be long. They'll wait for me.'

I watched him walk back along the boat and cross the thin plank to the riverbank. I lost him in the crowd, catching fleeting glimpses among the faces. The engines of the boat roared into life. Puffs of black smoke rose into the air.

'Noy!' I yelled. I saw him again, beside a rice stall. I stood up and leant out of the boat. 'Noy!'

I glanced to the back of the boat to see the captain pulling up the plank.

'Noy!' I yelled.

But Noy wasn't buying rice. He was standing in the road waving his arms, but not at me. A motorbike veered through the crowd and stopped beside him. The rider's face was hidden beneath his visor. Noy swung his leg over the motorbike and clung to his back.

Noy looked round once. His eyes locked onto mine and I couldn't tell if it was regret or goodbye, but in that one moment, in that fleeting second, I understood.

Moon Bear

I knew I would never see Noy again.

I sat back down and felt a pit of sickness rise from deep inside me. I reached into my bag for the honey-tin. But I didn't even need to look. I already knew what I would find.

I opened the tin.

The empty space stared back at me.

The money.

All of it.

Had gone.

CHAPTER 27

A fine rain was falling as the longboat pulled up at the nearest town to the village. The hills and limestone peaks of the mountains that had lined the last two hours of the journey were veiled from view. I was glad of the rain. It hid me too. I was returning with no money, and I wondered what Ma and the villagers would think of me.

The village was quiet as I entered. Children I didn't recognize stood beneath the stilts of their houses, their big eyes watching me pass. An old man leant on his stick. He wasn't from our village either. I wondered how many new people had moved here too. What if my village had been moved on again? I felt like a stranger here. Dogs barked but didn't leave the shelter of their dry spots beneath the houses. I looked back at what had been the chief's house but the shutters were closed against the rain. There was no sign of Noy's brother.

The mud was slick and red. It squeezed over my flip-flops and between my toes. It was hard walking, trying to keep the bag with Ma's silks out of the mud.

And then I saw them. 'Sulee!' I shouted 'Mae!'

Sulee turned. She grabbed Mae and stared at me, open-mouthed.

'Sulee, it's me,' I yelled. I started running towards her. They ran to me too and I was on my knees, my arms around them, and their arms around me. Mae buried her head into my neck and I felt home again.

'TAM!'

I looked beyond my sister to see Ma running down the road towards me, her skirts flying out behind her.

'Tam!' She crumpled down beside me in the mud and put her hands either side of my face and pressed her forehead against mine. She stared deep into my eyes and didn't wipe the tears that fell down her face. 'I thought I had lost you.'

I put my hands on hers and smiled. 'I promised I would come back.'

Ma traced her fingers across my face and nodded. She turned to Mae and Sulee. 'Go tell everyone that Tam has returned. Come,' she said. 'We have much to celebrate. My son has come home.'

I walked with Ma back to the house. I was relieved to see she had been allowed to keep the house given to her when we moved to the village. In the time I'd been away, Ma seemed older. Fine lines now crinkled across her face where she had smooth skin before. I felt older too, by years rather than just months. There seemed a whole world between me, and the boy I used to be.

'Sit down,' said Ma. She fussed around me, finding me a soft rug to sit on. She lit the small stove and put a pan of water on to boil. The room was dark inside, the shutters closed to keep out the rain. Ma pulled a bunch of herbs from a basket and started chopping them on a board. I smelt the fresh scent of mint fill the air. I had so much to say, too much. My mind ached with lack of sleep and the exhaustion of just being here. I was safe here. I could sleep and wake knowing I would be with my family. I could tell Ma sensed this too. She just let me sit with my thoughts in the darkness while she chopped and prepared the food. The fresh tang of lime mixed with mint and coriander and the salt scent of fish paste. Mrs Sone's food was good, but Ma's cooking was the taste of home.

I felt my head drop and my eyelids close. I was aware

of footsteps on the wooden steps outside. The door swung open and I lifted my head.

A man stood, silhouetted in the doorway, his wiry frame blocking the light. 'Tam?' he said.

I rubbed the sleep from my eyes and stared at him. 'Pa?'

The man knelt down beside me, and only then could I clearly see his face. 'Grandfather?' I said. I reached out to touch him, to make sure it was him, to make sure he was real. 'What are you doing here?'

Grandfather studied my face before he spoke. 'I came when I heard about your father,' he said.

'How did you hear?'

'The men at the logging station told me when I was trading forest meat. I came back to help your mother.'

Ma opened the shutters. 'Look,' she said. 'The rain has cleared.'

A pale sun shone through the golden mist left by the rains. Mae and Sulee burst through the door.

'The chief is on his way from the fields,' Mae said.

Ma poured two cups of hot water infused with mint leaves. I sipped mine and stared into the steam.

'Noy told me you didn't get any of the money I earned at the bear farm,' I said.

'Noy?' said Grandfather. 'You have seen Noy?'

I bit my lip and stared into my cup.

'Tam,' he said, 'I think you have a story to tell us, and I think that we should hear it all.'

And so I told it. All of it. About Kham and his family and about the Doctor and about the bears. I told them about General Chan and his daughter too. They laughed when I told them about the lady-bear in the city. I told them about all the money I'd earned with Sôok-dìi. When I got to the part about Noy, I stalled. I said we'd met and that Noy was going to come back with me.

'But he didn't,' said Grandfather.

'No,' I said.

'But he wanted the money?'

I folded my head onto my lap. I didn't want him to read my face and see the truth. I didn't want them to know Noy had taken all the money, but Grandfather guessed it anyway.

Ma sat down next to me. 'It's not your fault, Tam,' she said. 'You are here. That is what matters now. It is enough that you have brought yourself.'

'I have these for you though,' I said. At least I wasn't empty handed.

Ma opened the bag. She ran her fingers along the bolt of silks in red and gold and forest green. 'These are beautiful, Tam,' she smiled. 'I will be able to make much for the tourists and the markets with these.'

I handed the two dresses to Mae and Sulee and they ran off to try them on.

Ma filled my cup again. 'Drink up, Tam. The villagers will be here soon to welcome you back home.'

People crowded into our house. Women admired the silks and cloths I'd bought for Ma. As darkness fell, more people brought drink and food and it turned into a party. We waited for Noy's brother to arrive so that he could perform the Baci ceremony, of tying white cotton around my wrists to keep my souls safe inside. In truth I felt they'd stayed close beside me all the time. Grandfather opened a jar of rice whisky and handed it around the adults. Mae and Sulee curled up against me and fell asleep. Ma wouldn't leave me alone. Although I wasn't home in the mountains, I felt I was home with the people I belonged to.

At the end of the evening Noy's brother slid down next to me. His eyes were glazed from whisky. I noticed Grandfather looking our way. Noy's brother was only three years older than me, yet now he was the chief.

'Tam,' he said. 'Did your grandfather say that Noy left us?'

I looked at Grandfather.

Noy's brother took another swig of whisky. 'Noy wanted to make his way in the city.'

I stared at my hands.

'I thought he might have tried to find you.'

I looked up, 'Me?'

Noy's brother nodded. 'He wanted what you had. He wanted to be his own man and work in the city.' He leant back and stared up at the ceiling. 'It was never enough for him here.'

'I want to be here,' I said.

Noy's brother sighed. 'For Noy, the rice grows better on the other side of the river.' He searched my face for news. 'Have you seen him?'

'I haven't,' I lied. I stared hard at the space between my feet, at the circular knots of wood. I hoped Noy's brother wouldn't see through my lies. But maybe he had too much rice whisky to notice.

He leant back and sighed. 'Then we must hope that like you, he will come back to us one day too.'

I glanced sideways at Noy's brother. He was no longer the boy who would be chief. He was just a boy searching for his brother. A brother, who I knew deep down inside, would never return.

Chapter 28

I woke to a breakfast of noodle soup and cold rice from the night before. I'd slept deeply through the darkness and silence of the village night, woken only by the cockerels and the village dogs. Grandfather wiped sticky rice around his bowl and licked his fingers clean. 'Tam,' he said. 'I think you and I should go to the rice fields today.'

I looked at Ma. I didn't want to go. I didn't want to go back to the place where Pa had died.

'They cleared the bombies,' said Ma. 'It's safe now.'

'I know,' I said.

Grandfather stood up. 'Come with me, Tam. Maybe it will not feel so bad after all.'

I followed him out of the house and we walked along the road, up towards the paddy fields. Sulee and Mae followed. Ma had dug a small vegetable garden and herb patch in the land behind our house. I could see the stalks of lemongrass and the deep greens of coriander and the deeper green of mint.

People waved from their houses and vegetable plots.

'There are new people here,' I said.

Grandfather nodded. 'After the sickness, another village was moved to join this one.'

'Does everyone get on?'

'Most of the time,' said Grandfather, 'although Noy's brother and the other village chief do not always agree. Their chief is older and likes to get his way and Noy's brother is still young.' Grandfather smiled. 'He has time to learn.'

I stopped at the foundations of the school General Chan had proudly shown us. Grass and weeds crept across the concrete base.

'General Chan promised us a school,' I said.

Grandfather walked on. 'General Chan promised a lot of things.'

I jogged to catch up with him.

'The teacher left because she was not paid,' he said. 'She never came again. When we asked for doctors, they sent one, but two weeks too late. General Chan promised extra rice, but it never came. You cannot eat promises, Tam.'

We walked on in silence. The path curved upwards to a long ridge and to our paddy fields. The sky was a deep blue, the hills a smudge of green.

'You were right, Grandfather,' I said. 'We should have stayed in the forest. One day we will go home. All of us. We'll go back to the forests.'

Grandfather sighed. 'Soon there will be no forest, Tam.'

I stopped and he turned to face me. 'No forest?'

'The logging company cleared the hillsides on a scale I had not thought possible. You would not recognize it now. They are going deeper and deeper in.'

'But they were only building a road,' I said. 'Why do they clear the forest to build one road?'

Grandfather looked at me. 'Tam, trees are money. They are cut and loaded onto lorries for Vietnam and China, America and Europe. I saw it with my own eyes. We may have no home to go back to.'

I stared hard at the red earth beneath my feet. No forest? No home? What about Sôok-dìi? How would I get him home? Surely there must be forest higher in the mountains.

'Come,' said Grandfather. 'Let me teach you how to farm lowland rice.' He smiled, showing his teeth, red from years of chewing betel nuts. 'I am learning and I am an old, old man.'

I had dreaded walking up onto the ridge and seeing the field where Pa died. But it had changed so much since then, that it seemed a different place. The fields were thick with growing rice. There were a few people in the fields, their wide-brimmed hats keeping off the sun. A few children ran around knee deep in waters with tins full of frogs they'd captured for their supper. Mae and Sulee ran off to join them too. Beyond our field, I could see fruit trees planted on the low rise of the hill.

'They will not fruit for another year,' said Grandfather, 'but in two or three years, there will be a good crop.'

'Pa thought we would keep bees,' I said. 'He said we'd keep them beneath the fruit trees and collect their honey and sell it to the markets.'

Grandfather rubbed his chin, but didn't answer.

I looked across the rice field to see Mae and Sulee bent double over the water. What if there were still bombs here? What if there were some that hadn't been noticed? I clenched my hands in tight fists. Sulee plunged forward in the water and held up a frog.

Moon Bear

I couldn't help grinning. Mae took it from her and put it in their jar and they both went back to frog hunting again.

That night I sat with Ma and Grandfather and Mae and Sulee outside our house. We ate rice and salad and frogs on sticks. The lamplight burned low and soon fizzled out. We sat beneath a full moon, so bright it seemed almost like day.

Ma pushed more rice towards me. 'Eat up, Tam. You must be hungry.'

I rolled another ball of rice in my palm, but my throat felt dry and clogged. 'I must go back,' I said. 'I must go back on the first boat at dawn.'

Ma stopped eating.

Grandfather looked between us. 'There is no need, Tam. The Doctor is a greedy man who does not pay you. You are better off here where you can help in the fields.'

Ma nodded. 'There is nothing for you there.'

I closed my eyes and thought of Sôok-dìi, his nose pressed against the bars, waiting for me. I thought of him trapped inside his cage and the Doctor using him for his bile. I thought of the life he'd never have. I thought of the promise I'd given him.

I put my rice down and looked up at Ma. 'I have no choice,' I said. 'I must go back.'

CHAPTER 29

It was hard leaving Ma and Grandfather and my sisters, but it would have been impossible to stay. Ma was angry. Mae and Sulee were crying and holding on to me, but I think Grandfather understood. He walked with me to the Mekong and stood watching as the riverboat slipped out into the river and into the swirl of downstream currents. I watched him until the boat turned a curve in the river, and forests and high mountains surrounded us. There were still forests, I said to myself. And somehow I would make sure Sôok-dìi made it back.

The riverboat didn't arrive in the city that night. The engine kept stalling and we limped into the city the next day at dawn. I raced through the streets. If the Doctor arrived early, he'd be mad if I wasn't there. I ran past the monks collecting alms, and through the maze of stalls setting up for market.

I was relieved to find the gates of the bear farm locked. The Doctor hadn't arrived. I grabbed the keys from my room, where I'd asked Kham to leave them, and slipped through the gates, closing them behind me. Inside the barn the bears hooted and scuffled in the darkness. Kham said he'd feed the bears but they wouldn't have been cleaned out since I left and I knew there would be mess. It couldn't be helped. I just hoped I could clear some before the Doctor arrived. I flicked the lights on and stared around. Kham hadn't only fed and watered the bears, he'd cleaned them too. The barn was spotless.

Sôok-dìi hooted and spun in his cage when he saw me. He pawed at the bars, trying to squeeze his way through. I wanted to let him out and let him charge around in mad circles, but I knew the Doctor could come in at any second. I scratched Sôok-dìi on the head and around the ears and he turned over, letting me run my hands across his belly. I reached into my pocket for the small papaya Ma had given me. I'd saved it for him.

Sôok-dìi nosed in my hand.

'Mountain Boy!'

210

Moon Bear

I turned my back to Sôok-dìi and hoped he'd eat the fruit without the Doctor noticing.

But the Doctor wasn't interested in Sôok-dìi. He turned to Biter and bashed his metal bar against the cage. Biter threw himself at the bars, snarling and clawing at the Doctor. 'General Chan is coming today,' the Doctor said.

I wasn't sure if he was talking to me or to Biter.

'So we must be ready.' He bashed the bars again and Biter growled. 'We must be ready to show we have the strongest bear.'

Asang entered carrying a sack of rice. 'General Chan is here already,' he said.

I looked beyond him through the sliding doors into the yard. General Chan had arrived. It was early for him. The morning still had the first cool of the day. I saw his daughter get out of the car too. I looked for her friend but couldn't see him.

'My daughter is very sick,' I heard the General say.

The Doctor bowed. 'I am very sorry.'

General Chan wiped his face with his handkerchief. He paced around, his face hot and reddened. 'You said yours was the best bear bile.'

The Doctor smiled. 'But of course.'

'Then why,' scowled General Chan, 'is my daughter getting sicker?'

The Doctor smiled again and bowed his head, but I could see his knuckles whiten as he clenched his hand around the iron bar. His eyes darted side to side.

'My physician says that I should look elsewhere for bear bile. He says these bears are old and that you milk them for their bile far too often.' General Chan held up a vial to the light. 'See,' he said. 'It should not be dark and sludged like this.'

Out of the corner of my eye, I saw Savanh climb out of the car. The driver helped her out and she edged across the yard. She looked frailer than I'd seen her. Her skirts flapped loosely around her thin legs.

'Please come this way,' said the Doctor. 'See here.' He banged the bar against Biter's cage. Biter snarled and lashed out. 'See we have the strongest bear.'

General Chan snorted. 'This bear is old. He has no teeth or fur to speak of. He knows how to snarl but that is all. I know many men like that, all cowards.'

'I have many bears,' said the Doctor. 'Maybe you would like to try another?'

General Chan's eyes came to rest on Sôok-dìi. 'What about this one?'

Moon Bear

I felt my heart thump in my chest.

'He is too young.' I blurted the words before I could stop them.

The General turned to look at me. He frowned. 'The Bear Boy from the forest!'

I stared at the floor and wished I had said nothing. So he did know who I was.

'Has this bear been milked before?' asked General Chan.

The Doctor looked between General Chan and Sôok-dìi, as if trying to work out the right thing to say. 'This bear is young and healthy,' he said. 'No one has yet tasted his bile.'

General Chan rubbed his chin and nodded. 'Then this is the one.'

Sôok-dìi had finished his papaya and was pushing his nose through the bars. I felt sick. I wanted to take him away right then. I wanted to unbolt the cage door and take him and run.

'A good choice,' said the Doctor. 'Asang,' he shouted. 'Take General Chan to the milking room and get the pumps and ultrasound ready. We will milk the cub.'

I watched General Chan follow Asang and the Doctor to the treatment room. I put my hands on the lock to

Sôok-dìi's door. Maybe I could just go. We could leave right now and earn our money on the streets. I pressed my head against the bars and Sôok-dìi pushed his tongue out and licked my forehead. But I knew it was no good. The Doctor would find us and I wouldn't see Sôok-dìi again.

I heard the Doctor's footsteps and turned. He was walking towards the cage with a syringe and his metal bar in hand. I faced him, my back to the cage door.

'This bear is too young,' I said. The words sounded loud and more confident than I felt inside.

The Doctor stopped, syringe in hand, and stared at me.

'He is too young,' I said.

The Doctor spat on the floor. He jerked his head. 'Move away, Mountain Boy.'

I spread my arms out across the bars. 'No.'

The Doctor clenched his jaw. A small blood vessel pulsed on the side of his forehead. He took one look behind him, towards the closed door of the milking room, and stepped forward. 'Move away, Mountain Boy.'

I gripped onto the cage, holding myself against it. I saw the metal bar and then lights. An explosion of lights inside my head. An explosion of pain. I felt my legs buckle and I fell in slow motion, my head tipping back and back and back, until I felt the crack of it hitting the floor. I could feel warm blood seep through my hair. The last thing I saw was the Doctor standing over me, Savanh watching, hidden in the shadows, and bright stars spiralling into darkness.

When I woke, one eye couldn't see. I was flat on my back on the concrete. I looked through the other eye through a haze of red. I looked up to see Sôok-dìi's cage door wide open and empty. I tried to lift myself from the floor but nothing would move. My body didn't feel mine at all. It felt heavy, useless, pressed against the ground. I turned my head and saw Biter in his cage, watching me, his dark eyes fixed on mine. It seemed we watched each other for a long while. It was almost as if I could feel him, somehow, as if he was saying get up, get up and fight again. Never give up. Never. I could hear his breath whistle through his nose. I tried to lift my head, but the pain shot through me and I let the darkness wrap around me again and pull me down.

'Tam!'

I woke again, to cold water on my face. I opened one eye and watched Savanh dab her hankie on the end of a water bottle and trace it around my face. She dabbed the eye that wouldn't open and I winced.

'Sorry,' she said. She ran her fingers all around my eye and across my cheek. 'I don't think it is broken.'

She helped to sit me up against the wall. I touched my face and felt the swelling across my eye. No wonder I couldn't see. I looked across to Sôok-dìi's empty cage.

'How is Sôok-dìi?' I said.

Savanh didn't answer. She lifted up my chin to wash the blood away. She smiled. 'You are a very silly boy. Do you know that?'

I didn't smile back. I pushed her hand away and stared down at my own blood soaking into the concrete, a dark crimson stain.

Savanh sighed. 'The Doctor is bigger than you, Tam. He is crazy too. What were you thinking? Why did you even try to stop him?'

'I had to,' I said. I spat a lump of blood from my mouth onto the floor. I looked up at her. 'Who will speak for the bears, Savanh? Who will speak for them, when they have no voice of their own?'

CHAPTER 30

'What happened to you?'

I'd tried to sneak across to my room but Kham's mother had already seen me. She called me into their kitchen. I tried to cover the swelling across my eye.

Kham looked up from his homework. 'Tam . . . your face!'

Mrs Sone took my arm and brought me under the light and touched around my eye. I winced. She yelled to her husband out in the yard.

I heard the clank of a spanner touch the floor and heard his footsteps come into the room.

'I'm fine,' I said. 'Just fine.'

Mrs Sone held my chin up to Mr Sone. 'Just look at him.'

Mr Sone frowned. 'Tell us what happened, Tam?'

'It was my fault,' I said. 'A bear knocked me.' I looked at Mrs Sone but I could tell she knew it was a lie.

Mrs Sone put her hands on her hips. 'Tam, who did this to you?'

'It was my fault,' I said. I stared at the floor.

Mrs Sone shook her head. 'I know who did this,' she said. She pulled a tray of fish from the fridge and sat down at the table. She waggled a knife at Mr Sone. 'It's just not safe there,' she said. 'He's gone too far this time. It's no place for a boy.'

Mr Sone sighed and wiped the oil from his hands. 'It isn't for us to get involved.'

Mrs Sone shook her head. 'We can't let him work there. Look what has happened. If it were Kham, what would you do?'

'The Doctor's father brings in half our work. It's not for us to interfere.'

'Mountain Boy!'

We hadn't heard the Doctor come to the door. Mr Sone fell silent and turned the oilcloth round and round his hand.

Mrs Sone glanced at her husband. 'What can we do for you, Doctor?'

Moon Bear

The Doctor looked at me and then at Mr Sone. He stepped across the room and touched my face with his hand. 'How is your face, after your fall?'

I stepped back. 'It is fine, thank you, Doctor, just fine.'

The Doctor smiled his thin hard line. 'Good. Well I have this for you.'

He handed me an umbrella, bright blue and laced with pink. 'It belongs to General Chan's daughter. She left it behind today and has asked it to be returned tomorrow morning to the house. The address is inside.'

I took the package and watched the Doctor walk away.

Kham's mother brought the knife down on the fish's head with a loud thwack. 'It's just not safe there. It's no place for bears either.'

That evening, I sat with Kham beneath a dome of light from the oil lamp he'd brought with us into the bear barn. Sôok-dìi wouldn't come out of his cage. He'd taken most of the day to come round from his deep sedation. He'd woken and stayed hunched against the back of the cage, showing the whites of his eyes and hooting at us when we tried to coax him out. He hadn't even touched the overripe bananas we'd pushed in for him. I'd lost his trust. It was as if he knew I couldn't protect him any more. Maybe he even thought I was the one to hurt him.

We sat in silence listening to the other bears munch and slurp on the fruits Kham had brought.

Kham picked at the loose sole on one of his trainers. 'Ma says it's wrong,' he said quietly.

I stared into the small flame, flickering on the thin wick.

'She was the one who cleaned the bears out,' he said.

I looked at him. 'Your ma came *here*?'

Kham smiled. 'She saw me sneak over and came to find me. She was going to stop me until she saw how the bears lived. She said it is no life at all for them.'

I sank my head onto my knees.

'I told her where you'd gone too,' he said.

'What did she say?'

'She thought you wouldn't come back. But I knew you would. I said you'd come back for the bears.'

I nodded. 'I had no choice.'

'So what will you do?' asked Kham.

'Do?' I said.

Kham leant forward and covered the lamplight a little with his hand. 'Tam,' he said, 'I know you cannot stay.'

Moon Bear

'No,' I said.

'And you will take Sôok-dìi.'

I stood up and tried to coax Sôok-dìi over with some rice crackers. He pressed against the bars, away from me. 'I want to take him back, Kham,' I said. 'To the forest.'

Kham's eyes widened. 'You can't just let him go, Tam. He hasn't learned to hunt or find food for himself.'

'I will help him,' I said. I felt hot tears burn behind my eyes because I knew what Kham was saying was true. 'I know the forests, Kham. I can survive in the forest. I have lived there all my life. I will teach him where to find the berries, to root for nuts and mushrooms and where to find the eggs of the ant nest in the trees. Sôok-dìi will learn from me.'

Kham sighed. 'And how will you get him there?'

'I don't know,' I said. I'd been turning this over and over in my mind. 'What about one of the logging trucks that come to your father's yard?'

Kham shook his head. 'How will you sneak him into the truck driver's cab? I think they might notice a bear!'

'Then I will take him up the river on a boat and he'll be my dancing bear.'

Kham stood up and looked in at Sôok-dìi too. 'Tam,' he said quietly, 'General Chan thinks this is the bear to cure his daughter. He is not the sort of man who will let this bear go. If you leave, he will find Sôok-dìi and he will find you too.'

CHAPTER 31

The next morning Sôok-dìi was back almost to his normal self. When I opened his cage, he was reluctant to jump down at first. He sniffed the air and looked around him as if the air were different in the barn. Biter was watching from his cage, his paws splayed to try to cool himself. It had been a hot and sticky night, one of the hottest since I'd lived here in the city. There was no getting away from it. No stream to wade through or mountain ridge to climb and feel for the breeze. Mama Bear's cub lay with his feet draped through the bars. His mouth hung open panting. I sprayed the hose on the bears to cool them, and Biter turned on his back to let me spray his belly with water. I wanted to reach through and touch him, but didn't dare. I'd seen just how fast he could move when he wanted.

Sôok-dìi followed me around, snuffling under the other bears' cages for dropped food and licking up the puddles. I rolled him onto his back and tickled his belly. When I traced my fingers along the needle marks in his skin, he tried to pull my hand away with his mouth. 'Come on,' I said. I kicked a tin can along the barn and he chased after it, patting it with his paws and scuffing it up into the air. I let him play while I fed the rice and water mix to all the bears.

I didn't have any money to buy fruit. I would have no money until Kham and I could take Sôok-dìi dancing for the tourists again, but I didn't know when that would be. I coaxed Sôok-dìi back into his cage with a piece of chicken I'd saved from my supper the night before. I shut the door and he pushed his big paw against the bars and tried to reach me. I slid his tray of rice into his feed bowl and watched as he licked and snuffled around his tray for every last grain of rice.

I wanted to stay longer and let him out in the barn to stretch his legs and play. I wanted to regain his trust. But I couldn't. I had to take the umbrella back to Savanh.

I picked it up where I'd left it on the office table. The umbrella was pink and blue cotton, edged with gold lace. It was more to keep the sun off than the rain. The handle was enamelled and painted with small birds flying in a pink sky against a canopy of green leaves.

I ran my fingers along the enamel and frowned. I felt a rush of anger in me. Who was she to demand that her umbrella be returned? She could have waited until her next visit, or asked the driver to come and fetch it, but no, she expected me to walk across the city to take her umbrella. What did it matter that she was pretty, or the daughter of General Chan? She had seen how the bears were kept and how they were treated. How could she take the bile? What made her think she was different?

I set off across the city with the umbrella, carrying resentment with me all the way. Kham's father had told me how to find the house. It was on the hill road that rose up from the sprawl of houses, shops, and warehouses that strung out along the outskirts of the city. The houses here were bigger, grander, set behind tall gates and walls. A breeze lifted up and carried over the great river plain and cooled the people in these houses. There were no potholes. The roads were paved and smooth.

I stopped at the end house in front of a huge pair of gates. I looked back across the city. A haze of dust hung above the rooftops. I followed the line of the Mekong winding its way north and south. I could see the distant ridge of blue hills and beyond, the hazy impression of the mountains. It felt as if I could see the whole world. I wondered if that's how the people in these houses felt. Maybe they could see the whole world and not feel trapped within the city.

I looked down at the umbrella in my hand. It was covered with a fine sheen of city dust. I tried to wipe it with my hands, but my hands were sweaty and smeared the pink cotton. I didn't care anyway. For all I knew Savanh might have hundreds of pink umbrellas, a new one for every day.

I reached up and rang the bell.

The wire grille next to the bell answered. 'Who is calling?'

I looked around. What should I say? 'I am returning an umbrella left at the bear farm.'

A pause. A buzz and a click. 'Push the gate and come to the main house.'

I pushed the gate and peered through. A wide paved drive ran up to a house with steps and pillars either side of the door. A gardener sweeping leaves leant on his brush to watch me pass. The garden was full of trees and flowers. Flame trees lined the drive, their fingered leaves bright against the blue sky. It would take the dry season to burst their orange flowers into flame.

Moon Bear

I lifted the knocker of the big door and heard the knock echo through a hall beyond. A woman in a silk black skirt and white shirt answered the door.

'I have this,' I said. 'For Savanh.'

The woman took the umbrella from me and held it by finger and thumb, as if it were a long-dead rat.

'Savanh left it, at the bear farm.'

The woman nodded and shut the door. I stood for a few moments, staring at the door, at the metal knocker, a carving of a tiger's face. Nearly two hours' walk across the city and not so much as a thank you. I turned and headed down the steps towards the driveway.

'Excuse me!'

I turned. The woman was running down the steps. She lifted her arm to wave to me. 'Savanh wishes to thank you herself.'

I looked beyond her, half expecting to see Savanh in the doorway too.

'This way, please,' she smiled.

I followed her around the side of the house along a path lined with bougainvillea. Savanh was sitting at a table, holding the pink umbrella to shade herself from the sun. A pale pink silk was wrapped around her head. She stood up when she saw me and smiled.

'Thank you, Tam.'

'It was no trouble,' I lied.

She reached up to touch the swelling on my eye. 'How is it?' she asked.

'Much better,' I said. Mrs Sone's herbs had taken the swelling down.

I had to look twice at Savanh. She looked different somehow, brighter. Her face was relaxed; the lines of tension had disappeared. The whites of her eyes had lost their tinge of yellow. It was hard to say exactly what was different, but she seemed more *real,* more *alive.*

'Come,' she said and put her arm out towards a gateway in the trellis of flowers. 'Walk with me. Walk with me and see the animals.'

I walked beside her through the gate and into gardens filled with trees and flowers and cages. There were so many animals: gibbons, tortoises, and cages of colourful birds I never seen before. A small, private zoo.

Savanh stopped by a pen. 'This is Lulu,' she said. 'She's a marbled cat. She was brought to my father as a young cub, found with a broken leg in the forest. Father paid for her leg to be mended, but she could not return, so we keep her here.'

I watched Lulu pace back and forth, the coloured

swirls and streaks of her patterned coat matching the dapples of sunlight.

Savanh swept her arm around. 'They are all rescued from the forest. Some orphans, some injured.'

Two spotted doves flew up to the back of the cage, beating their wings against the wire.

Savanh tilted her umbrella back to look at me. 'My father says he helped move your village from the forest.'

I watched the clouded leopard pace along the fence of her pen and flip around to pace back. Did Savanh think we'd all been rescued too?

We walked in silence until we came to the pen with Jean-Paul. I'd never seen a tiger before. Grandfather had told stories about them, of fire spirits who roamed the forests. I looked through the bars at Jean-Paul. He paced his cage. He was tall and skinny. His skin hung from his hips and shoulders, like an oversized coat. His fur was balding and the colour was a dull orange, not the firelight of Grandfather's stories.

Savanh pressed her head against the wire mesh and whistled softly. 'My father loves his animals,' she said. 'They remind him of the forests.'

Jean-Paul walked towards us padding on his huge paws. He rubbed his chin and head against the wire mesh.

Savanh reached through to scratch him along the length of his back as he passed. 'Father used to take me deep into the forests too, to the hills where he grew up as a boy. I walked with him along forest paths in the deep cool dark beneath the trees. I remember once seeing a butterfly dancing in a shaft of sunlight. After walking through the shadows, its colours seemed so bright.' She smiled. 'I think I love the forests almost as much as he does.'

I frowned. 'Then why does he want to cut them down?'

Savanh looked round at me. 'What do you mean?'

I pushed my hands into my pockets. 'The logging trucks came to our village.'

Savanh smiled. 'Only to cut a path for the roads for the construction lorries to reach the dam.'

I looked at her. 'Not just the roads. The hills and the valleys. They are stripping out the trees. There will soon be no forest left.'

Savanh flicked invisible dust from her silk trousers. 'You must be wrong. My father would not allow that.'

I looked at her. 'It is happening, Savanh.'

She straightened her back. 'And have you seen this for yourself?'

'My grandfather has seen this,' I said.

Savanh glared at me. 'Then you cannot know if it is true. My father would not allow the forests to be cleared.'

I met her gaze. 'My grandfather does not lie.'

Savanh stared at me then turned, spinning her umbrella as she walked away.

She stopped at the next cage and waited for me. A mynah bird clawed its way along the wire mesh, pushing its beak through for food. The gold collar of feathers around its neck was bright against the black feathers of its body. One wing looked broken. The tattered feathers hung low at its side.

'I have a dream,' Savanh said, 'that one day I will work on the dam projects with Father too. Our country has rivers and mountains. We have everything we need to make electricity. Clean energy too. Father says Laos will be the powerhouse of Asia. It will bring our country out of poverty. We will have schools and hospitals for everyone.' She turned to me. 'Surely you more than anyone have seen this for yourself.'

I thought of the bare patch of earth for the promised school. I thought of the sickness and of the unwatched TV.

I said nothing.

'What dreams do you have, Tam?'

The question took me by surprise. 'I have no dreams,' I said. I watched the mynah bird hop away across the ground dragging its wing in the dust. Maybe it is only the wealthy who can afford to dream.

Savanh smiled and touched my arm. 'You must want something, surely?'

'I want Sôok-dìi to be free,' I said, 'to feel the earth beneath his paws, to be able to see the moon at night.'

Savanh sighed. She turned back to Jean-Paul's cage.

'My father says he has never seen me so recovered after a treatment. The medicines the Russian doctors gave made my hair fall out, but look now!' She lifted a corner of the silk scarf around her neck. 'You see, even my hair is beginning to grow back. My father says your bear is a miracle bear.'

I looked at the sheen of fine hair at the nape of her neck. 'And you,' I said. 'Is that what you think too?'

Savanh sighed and pressed her head against the cage. 'I have good days and bad days with my illness.'

Jean-Paul flumped on his side, and stared into me with his gold eyes.

'I do not have so many good days any more,' she said, 'and when I do, my father holds on to them and doesn't want to let them go.'

Moon Bear

We stood in silence and watched a butterfly flit through a shaft of sunlight.

Savanh turned to me and smiled. 'But no one can hold on to days, Tam. The only thing we can hold on to is hope.'

Chapter 32

News spread about Sôok-dìi.
The miracle bear.

The Golden Bear.

The bear to cure General Chan's daughter.

Three weeks passed and Sôok-dìi was milked three times. Each time I could not watch. I waited until the end of each milking to scratch his ear and run cool water through his mouth. People came to see him, to buy his bile. They offered ten times the usual price, but the Doctor refused to sell it. He said it was for General Chan's daughter only.

The Doctor was happy though. He charged people to come and see the Golden Bear. Rumour spread it was lucky just to touch him. People came to buy bile from the other bears. The Doctor arranged a tour guide to come with minibuses full of tourists to see the bears and buy the bile products. Fresh bile, flakes, and powder. They couldn't get enough. The Doctor even painted the bars of Sôok-dìi's cage in gold and put his name on the cage.

Sôok-Dìi.

Good Fortune.

It would have been impossible to take Sôok-dìi to the city to dance, because the Doctor came to the bear farm every day. He'd made Asang make space for five more cages. Five more bears would join us soon and more were planned. The Doctor painted a golden bear on the big red gates. His farm became known as The Place of the Golden Bear.

'Mountain Boy!' The Doctor walked along the aisle of bears, his eyes darting between the concrete under the cages. He pointed to fresh mess beneath Mama Bear's son's cage. 'Clean this filth. It must be spotless here today.' He rubbed his hands together. 'We have a very special guest. Dr Ho is a top Chinese medicine doctor. He is coming with General Chan and his daughter. Mr Ho wants to examine the Golden Bear and test the bile for himself.'

I sprayed water from the hose and watched the muck sluice along the concrete to the drain. The bears were restless. Jem and Jep swayed side to side. Biter pressed against the bars, growling. Spit and froth foamed around his lips.

But Sôok-dìi just lay curled up into the smallest ball as if he wanted to disappear, as if he hoped no one would see him or touch him. He moaned to himself, a low moan, his eyes tightly shut.

'Sôok-dìi,' I said. 'It's me.' I tried to scratch his ears, but he curled even tighter, tucking his head into his chest and would not be tempted with honeyed nuts or fruit.

Through the open doors, I saw two cars slide into the yard. Big sleek cars with tinted windows.

I turned off the tap and coiled the hose, looping it around the metal bracket. The driver of the first car opened the door and General Chan stepped out first, followed by Savanh and her friend, Talin. A short squat Chinese man stepped out from the second car. The Doctor rushed from his office to greet them, nodding and bowing to them. Savanh stood in the sunlight and opened her umbrella to shade herself from the sun. I watched her twirl it in the sunlight. I watched her laugh and tease her friend.

Asang passed me and pushed a bucket in my hand. 'The Doctor says you are to clean these flasks and tubes,' he said.

I looked in the bucket. The glass vials and flasks the Doctor used to collect the bile were green and sludged. It had not bothered the Doctor before. He just wanted me out of the way.

I nodded and took the bucket to the storeroom, a small room with a single tap and a drain hole into the concrete below. I sat on an old beer crate and gripped the bucket sides with my hands. I could hear the footsteps of the Doctor and of General Chan. I could hear their voices in the bear barn and the clatter of claws on the metal bars. I could hear Sôok-dìi hooting in fear.

I turned the tap on full and let the water rush into the bucket, splashing up the sides, a thunder of noise against the metal, a noise to drown out all other sounds.

I stayed in the store cupboard cleaning the flasks, removing every mark and blemish. I cleaned them again and again until I saw the Doctor and Asang return to push Sôok-dìi back in his cage. They left him splayed on the cage floor, his head and neck bent into the corner. I watched them walk away, back to the office, where the Doctor had laid out a spread of coffee and French cakes for General Chan and Dr Ho. I felt in my pocket for the almond biscuit I'd sneaked from the plate earlier for Sôok-dìi while no one was looking.

I opened the cage and tried to pull Sôok-dìi straight, but he was almost too heavy now. His mouth was dry and sticky. I poured a little water from a cup and he pushed his tongue forward and licked his mouth. It would be a while before he woke up fully. I gently ran my hands across his belly, across the soft skin shaved of fur.

I felt sick.

The Doctor must have had problems. Maybe he was nervous being watched by Dr Ho. I counted twenty red needle marks across his belly where the Doctor had tried to find the gall bladder. A clear yellow liquid trickled from one of the wounds. The skin on his belly was hot and tight, like a drum. Sôok-dìi groaned when I gently pressed it.

'Hello, Tam.'

I looked up to see Savanh standing next to me. She didn't look so well today. The filtered light through her pink umbrella cast a greenish shadow on her face.

I put my arm across Sôok-dìi, as if I was protecting him from her somehow.

She smiled. 'Can I touch him?'

I frowned. I didn't want her touching him. She was the one causing him this pain.

She looked at me. 'I hate this as much as you, Tam, but my father says bear farming in the city stops people catching wild bears,' she said. 'He says it helps conserve the wild bears.'

Moon Bear

I snorted and I glanced across at the new cages waiting for more bears.

'My doctors tell my father that I am getting better. They tell him this bear will cure me.'

I ran my fingers along the cracked skin of Sôok-dìi's paws. 'People tell your father the things he wants to hear.'

Savanh twirled the handle of her umbrella, twisting the top in a blur of pink and gold. She frowned, her eyes glazed with tears. 'Why would they do that?'

I looked at her. 'Because they are scared.'

Savanh raised her eyebrows and gave a small laugh. 'Scared? Of my father?'

I ran my fingers through the coarse hair on Sôok-dìi's back. 'Your father is a big man. People tell your father the things he wants to hear. They tell him that electricity has come to our village, that we have schools, that we have doctors. They tell him we are grateful to have been moved from the mountains. People are too scared to tell it how it is. They are too scared to tell the truth.'

I couldn't hide the bitterness from my voice. I thought of our broken village, not just broken from the mountains but people broken from each other. I thought of Noy and our broken friendship. I thought of the bears too, taken from their forests.

Savanh didn't say anything. She just stared at me, spinning the umbrella round and round in her hand. I couldn't tell if she was mad at me or not, but I didn't care.

'Sôok-dìi is sick,' I said. 'He will die.'

Savanh stepped forward and put her hand on my arm. 'Sôok-dìi is a fighter,' she said. 'I will see that my father makes sure he gets the best treatment.'

I pulled my arm away. 'You're the one making Sôok-dìi sick. Don't you get that?'

Savanh tried to pull me round. 'Tam . . . I wish . . .'

I spun round to face her. 'I wish you were dead.'

I felt Savanh's eyes on me for some time. Then she turned and walked away, her soft shoes padding on the concrete.

I trickled more water in Sôok-dìi's mouth. He was waking up slowly. His eyes twitched open and he blinked, watching me. I wished I'd said nothing to Savanh. It was a hurtful thing to say. I should have just let her stroke Sôok-dìi and go.

I slipped the almond biscuit from my pocket and crumbled it in my fingers, pushing the pieces in front of Sôok-dìi's nose. He snuffled them and reached out his tongue.

'I see you, Tam.'

Moon Bear

I spun round.

Savanh had returned and was watching me.

I hid the biscuit, shut the cage door and stared down at the floor.

Savanh walked up to me. 'I see you.'

'It's only a small biscuit,' I said.

Savanh leant against the golden bars. 'I'm not talking about the biscuit, Tam!'

I looked at her.

Savanh sighed. 'When I was little, I was a horrible child. Father used to bring home toys and dolls from his travels. Some of the dolls were so beautiful, dressed in silk. But I'd break them and throw them away. Some said I was spoilt. Maybe that is true. But I was angry. Angry that Ma had died. Angry that my father was often away. I would break the things he gave me. I'd take my anger out on those around me. I wanted him to die and have Ma back instead. I tried to hurt everyone I loved. My grandmother used to say, *I see you, Savanh. I see you.* She meant she could see into me, right into my soul and the person I really was inside.'

I ran my hands across Sôok-dìi's stomach, over the shaved skin. I traced my fingers over the reddened needle marks.

Savanh rested her hand on mine. 'I *see* you, Tam.'

'Savanh!' we both turned. Savanh snatched her hand away from mine. Talin was walking towards us. He glanced between us. 'Your father is looking for you.' He wrinkled his nose up at Sôok-dìi. 'Come, Savanh,' he said. He pulled her away. 'He's not clean.'

As I watched them walk away, I wondered if he was talking about Sôok-dìi or me.

I sponged water into Sôok-dìi's dry mouth and closed the cage door. He licked the water but didn't take the biscuit crumbs. His breathing was laboured, each breath ending with a grunt. I thought of Mama Bear, the night before she died. I felt his paws through the bars. Once soft and smelling of earth, they now were hard and cracked like the other bears'. His stomach was poked and riddled with needle marks, his fur coarse and bare where he'd rubbed himself against the bars. He'd lost his trust in humans. He'd lost his trust in me. It seemed the promise I had made him was as distant as the far mountain forests. Sôok-dìi was just like the other bears here.

Sôok-dìi was a farmed bear now.

CHAPTER 33

After the Doctor left, I stayed in the bear farm. I pulled up a stool and sat beside Sôok-dìi, stroking his head. He felt hot, his nose was dry and cracked. He drifted in and out of sleep. I left the barn doors open and watched the sky turn a fiery red.

Kham slipped through the gates.

'Tam?' he said, squinting into the darkness.

I waved him over. 'Is there a problem?'

Kham's eyes fell on Sôok-dìi. 'Ma wants to see you. Pa too.'

I frowned. 'What have I done?'

Kham shrugged his shoulders. 'Ma wants to see you now.'

'OK,' I said, 'but I must come back to sit with him.'

I closed the cage and followed him across the road into his

house. His father was sitting at the table and his mother was frying sweet coconut balls of rice. The smell of burnt sugar and coconut filled the room. She tipped them onto a wide plate, scattered some pieces of lime and put the plate in the middle of the table.

'Sit down,' she said.

I glanced at Kham and he sat down too. His mother pushed the plate and offered me one. I took one and looked between her and her husband.

She was the one to speak. 'Kham told us what happened to the money you earned.'

I looked at Kham. Had he told them about Sôok-dìi being a dancing bear?

His mother pulled some money from her apron and counted it out onto the table. 'This is for your journey back home.'

'Home?' I said.

She nodded. 'You must take this and go back to your family. I would say you could stay here, but it would not be good for the Doctor to see you around.'

I stared at the money. 'I can't,' I said.

She pushed the money towards me. 'Tam, I hear that General Chan's daughter has taken a turn for the worse.'

I looked up at her and tried to read her face.

Moon Bear

She sat down beside me and took my hand. 'When people realize the Doctor's bear is not a Golden Bear after all, the Doctor will not be a good person to be around.'

Kham's father was sitting watching me, slowly chewing his rice.

'I can't leave Sôok-dìi,' I said.

Kham looked at his parents. 'I told you he'd say that.'

His mother leant forward. 'Tam. It will not be safe for you to stay.'

I turned the rice ball round and round my hand, watching the grains of sticky rice glue together and reform in my hands. I couldn't eat. I put the rice down and pushed the plate away. 'Will you help me?' I asked.

They both looked at me.

I had to fight back the tears. Maybe this was my only chance. 'Will you help me to get Sôok-dìi away from here?'

Kham rolled his own rice ball round and round his hand. 'I told you he'd say that too.'

Kham's mother held my hands. 'General Chan is a powerful man. He still believes this bear will save his daughter, his only child. Anyone who tries to stop this would be in deep trouble.'

I clenched my hands together beneath hers.

She pushed my chin up. 'And anyway, where would we take him? We can't just release him into the wild.'

I looked at her. 'I'd look after him. I know the forests.'

She smiled. 'Tam,' she said. 'What sort of person would I be to send a boy off into the forest with a bear?'

I closed my eyes. 'He will die here,' I said. 'He will never know what it is like to be free.'

Kham's father leant forward. 'Tam,' he said. 'You must not stay here for the sake of a bear. This is not your battle.'

I sank my head onto the table. *But it is*, I wanted to shout. *This is my battle too.*

Mrs Sone was right. Savanh was sick again. She became too sick to come back again to the bear farm. Mrs Sone was right about the Doctor too. He took out his frustration on the bears. He thumped the cages with his metal bar, shouting at them and slamming the end of his bar through the cages onto their flanks. Asang followed behind, keeping his distance.

The Doctor came to Sôok-dìi's cage, leant against it and stared in. Sôok-dìi had curled up into a tight ball. He'd hardly eaten in the week since Savanh's last visit. He'd only taken some melon from me the night before. I'd seen the wound on his belly. The skin around it was crusty and hard. It was red and bleeding where Sôok-dìi had scratched it with his claws.

'Asang,' yelled the Doctor, banging the bars of Sôok-dìi's cage, 'we need to milk the Golden Bear. General Chan wants double the amount of bile today. He rang to say he wants the Mountain Boy to take it to his house today.'

I looked up. Why did General Chan want me?

The Doctor poked the end of his bar into a fresh pile of bear mess. 'Hey! Mountain Boy! Come here.'

I walked over to him, my palms slick on the broom handle.

The Doctor continued poking the mess beneath the cage. I could see the melon seeds in a pool of pale diarrhoea. 'What have you been feeding these bears?'

'I give them what Asang brings from the market,' I said.

The Doctor glared at me and spat on the ground. 'Fresh fruit? No wonder he's ill.'

I stared at Sôok-dìi and said nothing. To say sorry or to argue was to ask for another beating.

The Doctor turned back to Sôok-dìi. 'Mountain Boy. You will stay and help this time.'

I put the broom down and watched while Sôok-dìi was sedated and carried to the treatment room. I watched the Doctor stab him with the needle. The picture on the ultrasound scan wasn't clear. A white fuzz. The Doctor hit the screen several times but the screen didn't change. I watched beads of sweat form on his forehead and drip onto Sôok-dìi's fur. The Doctor breathed out a grunt of relief when bile started to flow through the needle and the tube into the collecting flask.

When no more bile would come, the Doctor held up the bottle. We could all see it was barely enough.

'Mountain Boy. Come with me.'

I followed the Doctor into the office. He pulled a stopper from a vial and added the contents of the flask inside. He sealed it with the golden seal of his farm, wrote a note and slid it into the envelope. He held the bottle just above my hand and leant forward. 'Why does the General want *you* to take this to his house?'

I stared at the bottle. 'I don't know.'

'You wouldn't be spreading lies about me, would you? Telling the General my bile is no good?'

'No,' I said.

I could feel the Doctor's eyes on me. He pressed the bottle into my hand. 'Take this to General Chan's house for his daughter. Tell him there will be more at the end of the week.'

I nodded and took the bottle from him, slipped it in my pocket and set out across the city. The sun was shining but the sky was metal blue, expecting rain.

I crossed the city and climbed the hill road. The distant hills were blurred by the coming storm. Savanh's house didn't seem so big and grand now. It reminded me of Sôok-dìi's golden cage. A show, a sham. I knocked on the door and was met by the lady who had opened it before.

'Please, come in. Savanh would like to see you.'

I followed her through the house, up marble steps and into a room overlooking the gardens and the animals. Savanh was propped up against cushions in a wide bed.

She smiled. 'You came. I asked my father's secretary to ask for you to come.'

I frowned. So it was Savanh who wanted me here, not the General. 'I brought this,' I said, holding up the small bottle of bile.

Savanh looked pale, her skin the blue-grey colour of rain-dampened wood ash. Her cheeks were hollow and she'd lost more weight just in the week.

She tried to raise herself up a little. 'How is Sôok-dìi?' she asked.

I put the bottle on the table beside her and went to stand beside the window. I stared down into the garden. 'He's not good.'

'You know,' said Savanh, 'I wanted a marbled cat so badly, that I begged and begged my father. When he brought me one as a kitten, he said he'd found it lost and wandering in the forest.'

I looked down at the marbled cat pacing in its world.

'Maybe you are right, Tam, and people tell my father things he wants to hear. But maybe we only hear those things we want to hear too. Sometimes the truth can be too hard to bear.'

I didn't know what to say. The storm-blue sky darkened the room.

Savanh leant forward. 'Tam, this bear cannot cure me. I know that. I think deep down my father knows that too, but he is a man who will not give up trying until the end.'

'Are you scared?' I said.

Savanh smiled. 'Maybe, a little,' she said. 'But I think of the time I walked through the shadows in the forest. It made me stop and wonder at those moments in the sunlight. It made me realize just how beautiful it was.'

Raindrops began to patter on the window. I watched them chase each other in crooked lines down the glass.

Moon Bear

'Tam,' said Savanh. 'There is something I wish you to do.'

I turned to look at her.

'I want you to take Sôok-dìi back to the mountains.'

'How?' I said. 'He is sick and your father would not allow it.'

Savanh pointed to a silk purse on her bedside table. 'Please pass it to me.'

I leant across and handed it to her.

'Here,' she said, pulling out notes of money. 'I want you to have this.'

I frowned. 'I don't want your money.'

'Take it, Tam,' she said. 'You may need it.'

I stared at the money in my hands.

Savanh pulled a mobile phone from her purse and started tapping on the keys. 'All this week I have been thinking of a plan to give Sôok-dìi his freedom. I want you to take Sôok-dìi and leave this city.'

I looked up at her. 'When?'

Savanh put the phone to her ear and smiled. 'You will leave tonight.'

CHAPTER 34

Savanh finished speaking on the phone. 'Talin will help you.'

'Talin? But he doesn't like me. He doesn't like bears!'

Savanh smiled. 'He says he will take you.'

I frowned. 'Why?'

'Talin and I are old friends. We go way back to childhood. He will pick you up at the bear farm at dusk tonight.'

'Where will he take me?'

Savanh slipped her phone back in her purse. 'I looked at some of my father's papers in his office and found where your old village used to be. Talin will take you as far as he can.'

I pushed the money deep in my pocket. 'I don't know how to thank you.'

Moon Bear

'Let Sôok-dìi feel his freedom.'

I just stood there, watching the patterns of light change on the walls as cloud passed overhead. A light breeze drifted through the room, bringing the promise of more rain.

Footsteps in the corridor outside broke the silence.

Savanh turned her head towards the door. 'It is my father coming,' she said. She reached under her pillow and pulled an envelope from under her pillow. 'Take this too. If my father finds you or stops you, give him this. Tell him it is a letter from his daughter.'

I stuffed the envelope down my shirt as General Chan walked through the door.

General Chan stopped and stared between us. 'Sa-vanh?'

'Father,' said Savanh. 'Tam has brought the treatment from the bear farm.'

General Chan glanced at the flask of bile on the table and then at me.

Savanh put her head on one side and smiled. 'Well, goodbye, Tam, and good luck.'

General Chan tucked the sheet around Savanh's shoulders and looked back at me. My head felt light and white inside. I wanted to say something. But the moment had gone. I turned and walked down the marble steps and into the pressing heat outside.

It was only then, I realized I hadn't said goodbye.

Back at the bear farm, I couldn't concentrate on anything. I kept out of the way of the Doctor. I hoped he wouldn't see my nerves. I hoped he wouldn't suspect anything. I cleaned the floors and the buckets. I brushed the yard and cleaned the toilets the tourists used. The late evening sun slid through a gap in the clouds and lit the rooftops in gold. I looked through the office window. The Doctor was still there. He didn't usually work so late. It was almost dusk. In my head, I was willing him to go.

Sôok-dìi had woken from the sedative, but he was dull and seemed thick with sleep. I wondered how easy it would be to get him to move. I wouldn't be able to carry him and I couldn't imagine Talin wanting to help either. I looked along the line of cages. Who would look after Biter and Jem and Jep, and Mama Bear's son and Hua and Mii? It would be hard leaving them. I wanted to take them all.

I left the farm to pack my things. I'd have to be ready to leave when Talin came for me. Kham followed me into my room.

Moon Bear

He watched me roll my clothes.

'You're going,' he said. It was a statement, not a question.

I pushed my clothes into the bag. 'I'm taking Sôok-dìi. I'm taking him to the forests.'

'How?'

I straightened up. 'It's better that you don't know,' I said. 'When I am gone, please thank your mother and father from me.'

Kham leant against the doorframe and let me pass. 'Come back one day, Tam. Come back and see us.'

I smiled. 'One day, Kham. Yes, one day.'

Kham switched off the light and we stood staring at each other in the dusk light. He slapped my shoulder. 'You'd better go,' he grinned, 'before Ma sees you and makes you sit for supper.'

I slipped out along the deep shadows and crossed the street. When I looked back, Kham was standing in a pool of light, watching me. I saw him wave and walk towards his house.

When I reached the bear farm gates, they were locked. The Doctor must have left. I took my keys and slipped through the gate. A light in the office was left on, but it was empty. I pushed open the door. Papers and a pack of newly

255

printed labels with a golden bear lay scattered on the desk. I opened the small cupboard and took a packet of the sweet biscuits the Doctor liked to eat. Sôok-dìi might need them later. I slipped in through the sliding doors of the bear barn and closed them behind me. I switched on the lights and the neon strips flickered into life. The bears shuffled in their cages, but settled when they saw it was me. Sôok-dìi lay in his cage, curled up, his paws wrapped around his nose. He groaned in his sleep. His breathing was fast and shallow.

I opened the cage and reached in. 'Sôok-dìi!' I ran my hands along his fur and tickled behind his ears. He wrapped his paws more tightly around his nose. 'Sôok-dìi, we are leaving tonight.' I waved a biscuit under his nose, but he didn't seem to want it. I raised my voice. 'Sôok-dìi!' I gave him a prod and he grunted and turned away. I'd waited for this moment for so long and now I couldn't get him out of here.

I paced up and down the cages. When would Talin get here? Would he even come at all? If he didn't, what then? I tried to shove Sôok-dìi, but he was too heavy to move. I slipped the head collar on him and tried to pull him round. In the next cage, Biter sat up. His ears swivelled towards the sliding doors and he lifted his nose to sniff the air.

'Psst! Tam.'

Moon Bear

I hid the biscuits under my shirt and walked to the doors. Talin was standing in the shadows. He shifted on his feet, looking back over his shoulder.

'Are you ready?' he said.

'Almost,' I said.

Talin wiped his sleeve across his forehead. His eyes flitted beyond me into the barn. 'I'll be parked down the street. When you come outside, I'll drive and pick you up.'

'I'll be there soon,' I said.

Talin nodded and turned. I watched him slip through the gates, closing them behind him.

I walked back to Sôok-dìi. 'Come on,' I said. I prodded him in his haunches. Come on, Sôok-dìi. You have to do this.'

He lifted his head and looked at me, then dropped his head on his paws again.

'Just one more time, Sôok-dìi,' I said. 'Please.' I reached into my bag for honeyed nuts. 'Hup! Hup!'

Sôok-dìi's ears pricked up, he shifted onto his feet.

'Come on,' I yelled. 'Hup! Hup!'

Sôok-dìi stood up and put his paws on the edge of the cage.

'That's it!' I scattered nuts on the floor for him to follow. He jumped down. I could see his legs were weak. He swayed as he walked, but followed me, his nose sniffing for more food. I slung my bag on my back and walked towards the doors.

The sliding door was ajar. Talin must have come back. His silhouette was framed against the doorway.

But it wasn't Talin.

It was the Doctor. He stepped out into the light, and whacked his metal bar against the nearest cage. The echo ran around the barn.

'Mountain Boy,' he said. He looked right at me with Sôok-dìi by my side. 'You're not thinking of going any-where, are you?'

CHAPTER 35

The Doctor slid the door shut behind him. He took a step forward. 'It's a good thing I decided to come back, isn't it?'

I backed away. Sôok-dìi stayed close, pressing himself against me.

The Doctor took another step, tapping the bar against the palm of his other hand. 'You are taking my bear. Maybe you think you can sell the Golden Bear for a good price?'

I shook my head.

'Did you think you could make money from my bear?'

I took another step back. 'I'm taking him to the forests. I'm setting him free.'

The Doctor stopped, his mouth curled in a smile. 'Free? Setting him free?'

The metal bar tapped against his hand.

'I'm taking him back and you can't stop me.'

The Doctor laughed. 'Brave words, Mountain Boy.' He leant forward. 'Or maybe just very stupid ones.'

I curled my fingers into Sôok-dìi's thick fur.

'Put him back in the cage, Mountain Boy, before I lose my temper.'

I stepped back towards Sôok-dìi's cage pulling Sôok-dìi with me as I went. The Doctor just stared at me. He clenched and unclenched his hand on the metal bar. 'Go on,' he said.

If I put Sôok-dìi back, I knew he would die. Maybe the Doctor would be so mad he'd kill me too.

Biter grunted in his cage. I turned to look at him. He was strangely still, watching us. He pressed his head against the bars and stared deep into me and held my gaze.

'Put the bear back,' the Doctor shouted. He was walking towards us now, banging the metal bar against his hand.

I reached up to Biter's cage instead. I unclipped the lock and turned to face the Doctor.

The Doctor stopped and stared. 'What are you doing? Don't be so stupid.'

I dropped the lock. It hit the ground, the sound of metal on concrete ringing out in the barn.

Moon Bear

I put my hand on the bolt.

The bar stopped tapping against the Doctor's hand. He stepped towards me, one step and then another, his eyes fixed on mine. 'Back . . . away . . . from . . . the . . . cage, Mountain Boy.'

I had no choice. I slid the bolt and swung Biter's cage door wide, wide open.

Time stood still.

We all stood still.

Except for Biter. He reached his nose through the opening and sniffed the air, then dropped down from the cage, his paws making no sound at all.

He was a big bear. He shook himself, shaking out the years of being trapped, unable to stretch or turn. He reared up on his hind legs, nearly twice as tall as me. I could feel him, smell him, and feel the heat from his own body. He'd be able to push me down with one paw. Sôok-dìi too. We were closer to him than the Doctor.

I held my breath and wound my fingers into Sôok-dìi's fur, willing him to be still.

Don't move. You cannot out-run, out-climb or out-swim a bear. You must become still. You must become like a spirit too.

The Doctor turned and ran. Biter let out a long snarl and exploded into a charge.

The last I saw of the Doctor, he was crumpled on his knees, Biter rearing up above him and pummelling him down.

I pulled Sôok-dìi through the doors and slid them shut behind me. The night air was hot and sticky. It pressed in, muffling the sound of the city, of radios and cars and motorbikes. If the Doctor died I'd be in big trouble and if he lived to tell the story I'd be in even worse.

I pulled Sôok-dìi out onto the pavement and scanned the road. Where was Talin?

Headlights caught us on the pavement and a white saloon car pulled alongside. The driver's window opened and a blast of cold air-conditioned air hit me.

Talin was in the driver's seat. 'Get in,' he said through gritted teeth. 'I have seen the Doctor walk along here not long ago. Get in.'

Talin looked more frightened than before. I pulled open one of the back doors. The white leather of the seats was clean and spotless. I threw some nuts along and half shoved and half carried Sôok-dìi in. He sprawled along the back seat, filling it. I slid in beside him and let his head rest in my lap. I had to move a bag of clothes from the back seat. They tipped out and I pushed a hat and long scarves onto the shelf behind the back seat.

'Don't let the bear get those,' said Talin. 'They're my mother's. She bought them on a trip to Thailand.'

I slammed the door as Talin's foot hit the accelerator and we lurched forward. He glanced back at me. 'This is my mother's car,' he said. 'Don't let the bear mess it up or I'm dead.'

I leaned back against the seats. They were soft and cool. Sôok-dìi was still. Too still. He felt hot despite the air-conditioning and his mouth hung open gulping air.

I watched the city pass in a blur of markets and buildings. It was the evening of the boat festival and people lined the streets, holding up candles in a river of light. Music pumped out onto the streets. I was glad that we could slide along with other cars, unnoticed. Talin's hands tightly gripped the steering wheel, his knuckles white. He pulled a cigarette from a pack on the seat beside him and lit it with the car's lighter. The coil of wire glowed red hot in the darkness of the car.

We soon left the city and climbed the hill road. I saw Savanh's house and wondered how she was. I almost wanted Talin to stop to bring her too, but he glanced once at her house and drove straight on. At the top of the hill, Talin had to slam his foot on the brake. A queue of cars snaked forwards.

'Trouble,' said Talin. He pulled on the cigarette and blew a steady stream of smoke. 'Checkpoint.'

Ahead, two soldiers were bending over checking cars.

I gripped my fingers into Sôok-dìi's fur. 'Have they heard about our escape already?'

'Doubt it,' Talin said. 'I think they're checking cars for smuggled goods for the festival.' He looked back over his shoulder as if looking for a way out, but several cars had pulled up behind us. Maybe it would be too obvious if we turned and drove away.

'Let's hope they only want to look inside the boot,' said Talin.

The car edged closer. I watched the soldiers opening car boots and checking cars. I had one idea, one plan and I didn't like to think what would happen if it didn't work.

Talin drummed his fingers on the steering wheel. He lit another cigarette and muttered to himself. In the rear view mirror, I could see the tight furrows in his brow.

'I'm sorry,' I said. 'I didn't want you to get in trouble.'

Talin didn't answer.

'Whatever happens, I want to thank you for doing this for Sôok-dìi.'

Moon Bear

'I'm not doing this for the bear,' snapped Talin. 'I'm doing this for Savanh.'

A soldier tapped on the window. It was our turn.

The soldier jerked his head to the back of the car. 'Open the boot.'

I breathed a sigh of relief. It gave some time for my plan at least.

Talin pulled the lever for the boot lock and I heard them walk behind the car and look inside. They slammed it shut and walked back to the window.

'Who are you travelling with tonight?' said the soldier.

Talin glanced back, but had to take a double look.

He turned to the soldier. 'I'm taking my cousin to see some relatives in the country.' He paused before he spoke. 'I'm taking my aunt too.'

The officer scanned the back seat with his torch. The beam lingered on me for a moment and then on a figure wrapped in scarves, a hat, and dark glasses.

Whether or not he saw an aunt or a bear dressed in finery on the back seat, he chose to believe what he wanted to see.

He tapped the side of the car with his hand, and waved us on.

CHAPTER 36

O nce beyond the city, the car fell into the steady rhythm
of the road, the hum of the engine, the rumble of
tyres on uneven tarmac, and the steady beat of Thai pop
music from the CD player.

It must've been like this that I fell asleep. I woke to
the car lurching over rough ground and rain hammering
the windscreen. The wipers thumped side to side. Pooled
water shlooshed beneath the tyres, spraying up against the
sides of the car. The headlights shone forward into reflected
raindrops, needles of lights firing at us in the darkness.

I didn't know how long I'd slept. I could only have
been asleep for a few hours but it felt like days. Judging by
the cigarette ends crushed into the ashtray it had been some
time. The air-conditioning had dried my throat and nose. I

Moon Bear

was cold too. It was like sitting in a freezer. I shifted in my seat and sat up. My legs were dead and cramped from Sôok-dìi's weight upon them. I felt his stomach. It had lost the heat and tightness, but Sôok-dìi groaned. Despite the cool air, he panted and grunted with each breath.

'You're awake.'

I could see Talin's eyes in the rear view mirror, watching me.

'How far now?' I said.

'Not far,' said Talin. 'We've been climbing for the last two hours. The roads are bad with this rain.'

I scratched behind Sôok-dìi's ear and he pressed into me, snuffling my hand for food. He licked the salt sweat from my fingers. His tongue felt paper dry and rough, like tree bark.

I stared back into the darkness. Far away, a pair of headlights appeared above us. They looked small at first, as if they were high in the sky. I watched them slowly descend. They slipped lower and lower, zigzagging back and forth. I could make out the edge of the mountain, high above us. I'd forgotten the mountains. I'd forgotten how vast and wild they were. It took a while for the truck to reach us. Talin pulled over to let it pass. It rumbled through, a monster truck, piled high with logs.

Somewhere out there were the mountains, tree covered, rolling back and back and back. I wanted to wind down the window and breathe the mountain air and let it fill me. I wanted to smell the trees and the rain and the wet earth. I wiped the sleep from my eyes. We'd soon be there. I'd managed to get Sôok-dìi to the mountains. Maybe he would feel better when he felt the earth beneath his paws. I tried to think of all the things I'd try to find for him to eat. It was the time of year for ant egg nests and wild fruits and mushrooms. Maybe there would be a late bees' nest to raid for honey.

Talin pushed on, up into the mountains, climbing up the road the truck had come down. If I looked out of the window beside me, I could imagine the road falling away into a deep void. The dirt road was pressed flat by the army of logging lorries.

The engine whined and strained as the car tyres struggled for grip in the mudded track. As the road levelled out, a faint line of dawn appeared on the horizon. The sky was clearing above. A crescent moon shone through a cobweb of thin clouds spanning out across the sky.

The logging station lay ahead, and beyond that the mountains of my home. The lights in the timber yards and from the workmen's houses glowed in the bluish light of

Moon Bear

dawn as workers woke for the day. I could see the flicker of the TV in the bar and already a few men sat on stools, beers in hand. The last time I'd been here was with Pa selling honey. A few people looked our way. I didn't want them questioning us, and neither did Talin. He drove on, fast along the road through the logging station and up into the hills.

I was going home, really home. I knew our houses wouldn't be there, but maybe I could build some form of shelter for myself. Maybe I could move deeper into the forest and when I'd settled I could bring back Ma and Grandfather and my sisters with me. I scrunched my hands into Sôok-dìi's fur. I'd promised him I'd bring him back. I promised that I'd make it happen. But all along it was Sôok-dìi who'd given me the courage to get here. He'd brought me here. It was Sôok-dìi who'd really made it happen.

As we snaked upwards into the first hills, I could see the loggers had been busy. The hills here were bare; the cut ends of tree trunks dotted the hillside. I fixed my mind on the forests beyond our old village. I knew those forests. I'd teach Sôok-dìi how to survive there. I could already see the ridge above us. Beyond that ridge, was home.

The road to the ridge was steep and rutted. The car's engine whined as Talin tried to push it on, but the tyres slipped and spun in the mud. Talin slowed to a stop and rested his head on the steering wheel. He looked tired. His white shirt was crumpled. Three empty packs of cigarettes lay on the seat beside him.

He turned to look at me. 'This is it,' he said. He glanced at Sôok-dìi spread out on the seat. 'This is as far as I can go.'

I nodded. I pushed Sôok-dìi from my lap and pulled the handle of the door. The cool dawn air swirled around us, damp from the heavy rains. 'Thank you,' I said.

I climbed out of the car. My legs were cramped and numb. I shoved Sôok-dìi and he raised his head. He sniffed the air, as if some long distant memory was stirring inside his brain.

'Come on,' I said. I scattered nuts on the seat to make him move, but he kept sniffing the air. He raised himself up and half jumped and half slid from the car. He pushed his nose on the red earth, snuffling and snorting at the mud, sending flecks into the air. I called him and turned towards the ridge.

Talin called me back. 'Tam, you forgot this.' He stood, the mud covering his white shoes, clutching my bag. Talin stumbled through the mud and pushed my bag in my hands. 'Look after him,' he said. He bent down and pushed

Moon Bear

his face into Sôok-dìi's fur. 'Look after him, for Savanh. Do it for her.'

I watched Talin walk back to the car and spin round, sliding in the mud. The red rear lights disappeared down the hill out of sight, leaving Sôok-dìi and me alone. I turned and started walking up towards the ridge. I could imagine the shape of the line of mountains beyond. I could imagine the deep forests.

'Come on, Sôok-dìi,' I said. 'We're going home.'

It took most of the morning to walk up the ridge. It became hot and humid. Airless. Sôok-dìi wanted to lie in the cool mud and sleep. I had to shove and pull him and tempt him with honeyed nuts. It wasn't far now. Beyond the ridge would be the forests with rain clouds misting in their branches.

A fine rain was falling as we neared the top. I dropped Sôok-dìi's rope and ran ahead of him, scrambling up on my hands and feet. I reached the top and stared around me. I recognized the contours of the land, the curves and twists of the mountains.

But there were no trees.

No forest.

CHAPTER 36

Nothing.

Just the bare red earth rolling endlessly back, pock-marked by cut tree stumps. Rainwater gouged deep gashes in the hillsides. Tree trunks lay on their sides like sun-bleached bones.

Grandfather had been right.

The forests had been cleared further than I could see.

There was no trace of where we once had lived.

There were no forests.

No trees.

No home.

I sank on my knees. I felt sweat trickle down beneath my shirt. Sôok-dìi curled up on the ground beside me. Rain began to fall faster all around us. Sôok-dìi's thick fur was clogged with mud and water. I ran my hands across his head. He closed his eyes. His mouth hung open, panting, as if he couldn't get enough air. I buried my head into the fur of his chest and lay like that, listening to his harsh breathing, listening to the beating of his heart.

I became aware of another sound too. A distant rumble. I looked up expecting to see one of the logging trucks, but the road leading up to the ridge was empty. The sound built up and filled the sky. A helicopter emerged from the thin mist. Sunlight glinted on its windows. I looked around but there was nowhere to hide, nowhere to take cover. The helicopter clattered out of the sky, circling the ridge.

Circling Sôok-dìi and me.

I sat up and wrapped my arms around Sôok-dìi. I felt sick inside. I knew who was in there. He had come for Sôok-dìi and I knew he would not let him go.

I held on to Sôok-dìi as the downdraught from the blades blasted in my face and whipped my hair. I watched the helicopter land and General Chan and two soldiers climb down. He pulled his suit straight and waded his way across the mud. A river of blood red earth ran between us.

General Chan stood over us. 'Did you think I wouldn't find you?'

I clung on to Sôok-dìi. 'He needs the forest.'

The General wiped sweat from his forehead. 'I need this bear.'

I gripped my fingers tight into Sôok-dìi's thick fur. 'Don't take him.'

General Chan signalled to the two soldiers. One pulled me away and I sprawled in the mud. I watched them reach down to lift Sôok-dìi. They struggled with him to the open side of the helicopter.

'General Chan!' I yelled.

He turned. Mud plastered his General's uniform.

I scrambled up and pulled out the envelope Savanh had given me. I pushed it in his hands. 'Here,' I said.

General Chan stared at me. 'What is this?'

'You must read it,' I said. 'It is from your daughter. It is from Savanh.'

CHAPTER 37

*D*earest Father
If you are reading this letter, you have followed Tam and the bear against my wishes. I ask again that you let them go, for it is not for us to think we own them.

Yet I know you do this just for me.

I see you, Father.

I see you in this darkness trying to reach me, trying to find a way to keep me with you. Yet, you do not see me. You see yourself alone, without Ma or me, and I know this scares you.

When Ma died, I was scared too. When you were away, Grandma took me for a walk through the forests. I wanted to stop and turn back but she said we must keep on walking. We walked through dark and deeper dark. My legs ached and I felt I could go no further, but still Grandma would not let me stop until we reached

275

the top of the mountain. I had never been able to see so far in my life. The mountains stretched for ever. Grandma said to me, 'Look, Savanh, do not forget there is a whole world out there for you.'

We sat together for some time looking across the mountains. When we stood up to leave I asked her what lay beyond the horizon, and she said to me, 'That is for us to imagine and walk towards there, holding the dream of what we hope to see and not to turn, however dark the path.'

Father, I dream of a land so rich and colourful with life for all of us. I dream of a land of a million elephants. I may not be able to make these things happen in my lifetime, but if Tam and Sôok-dìi return to their forests, then I have taken a few steps of the way.

So you must keep on walking too and know that I am with you.

If you look for me, you will always find me. I will be the butterfly that dances in the shaft of golden sunlight.

When you come looking, you will see me.

And I will see you too.

S xxx

Six Months Later

Sometimes when I look up at the stars at night, I look for the brightest star and think of Savanh. Maybe she is up there with Pa too. Ma says the people we have loved help us from the heavens. But I don't believe that now. I think what they did in life lives on within us, and within everything we do.

I shade my eyes and look up towards the mountain. The new Forest Reserve stretches all the way across to the other side. This is what Savanh would have wanted. This is what she made happen. The Savanh Chan Bear Rescue Sanctuary rests at the foot of this mountain surrounded by a backdrop of trees.

It took six months to build the complex of enclosures, the veterinary hospital, and the visitor centre. The sanctuary will open five days a week, for people to come to see the bears. The bear farm cages live in the museum now, holding only the ghosts of bears, together with the instruments of their torture.

The new enclosures back onto the forest. Most of the bears have lived their whole lives in the small cages and wouldn't survive in the wild. But here, they can smell the forest, hear it and breathe it. Their grass enclosures have trees to climb, pools to swim in, and toys of bamboo to play with. At night the bears can see the moon and stars. It's as close as they can get to freedom.

It is our home now too, for Grandfather, Ma, Sulee, Mae, and me. We live in a small village an hour's walk from here. Ma works for a textiles business run by other women. They even have a loom and plan to grow mulberry trees so they can keep silkworms and make silk.

Sulee and Mae love the new school, but it's not for me. I love days like this when I can go with Grandfather to see the bears, or walk with him inside the forest.

Grandfather is waiting for me by the entrance to the bear sanctuary with a basket of fruit for the bears. 'There you are,' he smiles. 'I have been waiting.'

I smile back. He looks so smart in his Forest Ranger uniform. Younger too.

Moon Bear

'Come,' says Grandfather. 'This is a special day. Let us go and see the bears.'

I walk with him through the entrance and along the paths bordered by flowers. It's the first week the sanctuary has been open for visitors and already it is busy. Another minibus with tourists has just arrived. I look inside the museum and see a party of schoolchildren crowding around the metal cages. One boy is allowed to climb inside. I watch him reach out to touch the bars, to feel how small it is inside.

'Kham came to see the bears last week,' I said.

Grandfather smiled. 'Did he want you to teach them all to dance?'

I grinned. 'No. He said he's got new plans. Better ones. He said one day he wants to create the ultimate wild-life experience for tourists and build log cabins in the forests and walkways through the canopies. He tried to get me to join him.'

'And what did you say?'

'I said I'd stick to bears.'

We walk towards the bear enclosures and stop at the first one. The shadows are deep and cool, the bears shaded by the forest. There are twelve bears here already.

I smile. I hardly recognize Biter. The vets thought he'd never be able to integrate with the other bears. After what he did to the Doctor, we all thought he'd be too vicious. The Doctor was barely alive when he was found. Kham's ma said he'd have been better off dead than in the state Biter left him, unable to walk or talk. But the strange thing is, since being here, Biter's one of the gentlest bears. He lies in the sunshine and swims in the pool. He's the first one to greet the new bears in the sanctuary.

Jem and Jep are here too. They roll and tumble down the slopes and stay curled together at night even though they must be three years old. Mama Bear's son shares their enclosure, though he likes to sit alone. In the daytime he stays curled inside his pen, but at night he likes to sit and stare at the moon. He's taken to one of the sanctuary staff, a grandmother with fifteen grandchildren. He follows her up and down the perimeter fence. She treats him like one of her own and gives him extra treats.

Hua and Mii are here. Their wounds have cleared and they have glossy black coats. Their pads have lost the thickened skin and they roll and play and climb trees, like wild bears of the forest.

Grandfather and I walk on until we stop beside an enclosure empty of bears. The rope hammock hanging between the trees lies unused. The water in the pool is still.

Moon Bear

I take a deep breath and stare around the empty space.

Sôok-dìi was not so lucky.

When the vets opened him up, he had an infection deep inside him. *Peritonitis* the vets called it. His body had shut down. They tried to keep him alive by flushing fluid inside, washing all the badness out. They pumped him full of antibiotics, but the vets said it would have taken a miracle for him to survive.

I press my head against the wire fencing of the empty enclosure and turn to Grandfather. 'Savanh said Sôok-dìi was a fighter.'

Grandfather smiles. 'Yes,' he said, 'and she was right. Look, here he comes.'

It's the moment we have been waiting for. His recovery has taken six long months. This is the first time Sôok-dìi will take a step outside. We see him, a dark shape at first behind the metal grille of the hatch to his outdoor enclosure. The hatch lifts up and he lifts his nose and sniffs the air. He takes a step onto the earth and presses his nose against it. He looks thin. His fur is patchy and ragged and his ribs and hipbones are visible beneath his skin. He sniffs again, smelling the other bears, and takes a step back inside.

I whistle to him. 'Come on, Sôok-dìi. You can do this.'

Grandfather opens the mesh gate to the enclosure. 'Maybe he'll come out if he sees you.'

I take a papaya from Grandfather and walk across the grass and crouch down next to the open hatch. 'Come, Sôok-dìi. It's me.'

I see him then, his black face and grey muzzle. He stumbles across in fast strides and throws his paws around my shoulders and nuzzles into me, making the deep humming sound in his chest. I push my face into his fur, but he's smelt the papaya and tries to take it from my hand.

I throw it away from me and it rolls a little way down the slope towards the pool of deep green water. Sôok-dìi shuffles down the slope, digging his claws deep into the earth. But he doesn't eat the papaya. He keeps on going, down towards the pool. He stops and sniffs the water, blowing bubbles across its surface. Floating leaves break up the sunlight. Sôok-dìi dips a paw in and then another. I watch him drop forward and slide deep beneath the surface. He comes up for air, blows a snort of breath and disappears again, leaving a ring of bright water. He surfaces and climbs out, shaking the water from his coat, scattering the sunlight. He shakes so hard that he falls over and lies on his back with his eyes closed and mouth so wide open that I almost think he's smiling.

Grandfather crouches next to me and puts his hand on my shoulder. 'Your father would have been proud.'

I look at the wire enclosures and the forest beyond. 'But the bears are still not free,' I say. 'Other bears will come. More will be captured from the mountains and more forests will be cut down. There will be more men like the Doctor and people who want to buy their bile.' I sink my head onto my knees. 'What hope is there for the bears? This is only one small mountain.'

Grandfather wraps his arms around me, and smiles. 'Tam, you are like Nâam-pèng.'

I frown at him. 'Nâam-pèng?'

'Do you not remember, Tam? Nâam-pèng, the smallest bee?'

I push Grandfather's hands away. 'What of him?'

Grandfather sweeps his arms across the bear sanctuary, across the trail of schoolchildren, families and the tourists. Sunlight glints from the windows of two more tourist buses climbing the steep road of the valley. 'Look around you, Tam,' he says. 'Do you not see what is happening here? Look at the people that have come here to find out about the bears and the forests. More will come and see this for themselves. They will want to change things too.'

I shade my eyes against the sun to see all these things.

'Listen, Tam,' says Grandfather. 'You are not alone. Do you not hear the bees?'

Dear Reader,

The idea for this story started swirling around in my head after reading a magazine article about the cruel practice of bear bile farming. I was shocked to learn that across South East Asia, many bears are confined in small cages, with just bare bars beneath their paws. They suffer hunger, thirst, and disease. They are subjected to painful and stressful procedures to extract their bile. They cannot behave in any way that is innately 'bear'. This is for the production and collection of bear bile for the traditional Chinese medicine market, a market with consumers all around the world.

I felt there was a story wrapped up inside one of these bears. I felt that one of these bears' stories needed to be told, and so I began to ask many questions: Where do these bears come from? Who captures the bears and who sells them? Who owns them? Who looks after them? Who milks them for bile? Who buys the bile? I noticed that most of my questions began with . . . "who?", and so it became a story about many people's lives. It became Tam's story too, and how he, like the bear cub, is taken from his forest home.

I also drew into this story the US bombing of Laos (1964-1973) during the Vietnam War. Millions of unexploded bombs remain in Laos today, littering the countryside and villages, putting lives and livelihoods under threat. In this story, Tam's life is turned upside-down when one of these bombs explodes and kills his father while out digging the fields. I wanted this part of the story to show that decisions made by governments around the world have huge impacts on future generations.

The big decisions facing us today concern the natural world, a world under threat from destruction and exploitation. When governments and global companies ignore these concerns, it seems impossible for our voices to be heard. Yet, I wanted to end the story on a message of hope and show that like the story of Nâam-pèng, many voices can bring about change.

To see what you can do to help end bear bile farming go to the kids' section of the Animals Asia website (http://www.animalsasia.org/eng/kids/index.htm).

I hope that you've enjoyed reading this story and know that you too, can really make a difference.

Gill Lewis, 2013

AMAZING MOON BEAR FACTS

1. Moon Bears get their name from the V-shaped patch of cream-coloured fur on their chest. This shape looks like a crescent moon.

2. In the wild, Moon Bears eat bee hives, fruits, nuts, insects, vegetables, and small animals like mice or birds.

3. It is said that bears can smell honey from a distance of five kilometres!

4. After their birth, the baby bears stay with their mother for up to three years.

5. Moon Bears tend to sleep during the day and are often awake during the night. They are at their most active at dawn and dusk.

6. Moon Bears are medium-sized bears, typically between 4-6 feet tall. Female bears are smaller than males.

7. In the wild, Moon Bears can live up to 30 years. On bear farms, many die at less than half that age, between 10 and 12 years.

8. Moon Bears are one of eight different species of bear in the world. The others are: American Black Bears, Brown Bears, Polar Bears, Giant Pandas, Sun Bears, Sloth Bears, and Spectacled Bears.

MOON BEARS ARE FOUND THROUGHOUT SOUTHERN ASIA

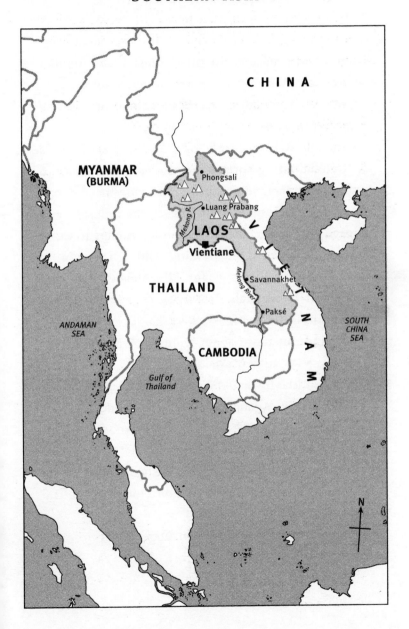

Acknowledgements

Huge thanks must go to Jill Robinson, the founder of Animals Asia, who generously gave her time to answer my many questions about moon bears and the bear bile industry.

Animals Asia not only operates bear sanctuaries for rehabilitating farmed bears, but also works to reduce the demand for bear bile, monitor the bile trade, increase public awareness of the industry, and engage with governments and policy makers to build support to end bear bile farming. Through promoting compassion and respect for all animals, staff and volunteers of Animals Asia work tirelessly to bring about long-term change.

To find out more about Animals Asia, visit their website: www.animalsasia.org.

I'd also like to thank Victoria Birkett of the Miles Stott Literary Agency and all the team at OUP, especially Liz Cross and Claire Westwood for their editorial surgery.

Thanks to Mark Owen for the wonderful inside illustrations and to Simon Mendez for the beautiful cover.

Biggest thanks as always to Roger, Georgie, Beth and Jemma.

Gill Lewis spent much of her childhood in the garden where she ran a small zoo and a veterinary hospital for creepy-crawlies, mice, and birds. When she grew up she became a real vet and travelled from the Arctic to Africa in search of interesting animals and places.

Gill now writes books for children. Her first two novels, *Sky Hawk* and *White Dolphin* published to worldwide critical acclaim and have been translated into many languages.

She lives in the depths of Somerset with her husband and three children and writes from a tree house in the company of squirrels.